Battles of Azriel
LOST WORLDS

Book 1: Ariella

DANICA PECK

Battles of Azriel: Ariella
BOOK 1
LOST WORLDS

DANICA PECK

Lost Worlds

Copyright © 2016 Danica Peck

Published by Ouroborus Book Services via IngramSpark
www.ouroborusbooks.com.au

Dedicated to Alexandria and Elliott,
My beautiful newlywed best friend, may you forever
find your happy ending.

Unclaimed Lands
Ghost Territory
Vampire Territory
Dark Elf Territory
Werewolf Territory
Underland
Alesmera
Ilyragasia
Meradom
Dragon Territory
Hollows
Mountain Falls
Kirravigne
Meyenae
Mystique
Kierra
Robin Falls
Starlex
Versattali
Krypto
Skarsgard
Alegesia
Katalina
Meranque
Saberial
Utia
Lyndittra
Azriel - the world of five kingdoms

CHAPTER ONE

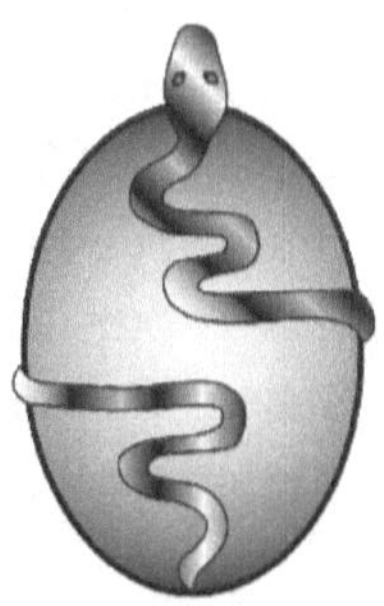

A silent, starless night echoed above a simple suburb hosted with small, brick townhouses. The wind blew a cold, harsh breeze through the trees that left the fallen leaves dry. Footsteps broke the silence; she looked around cautiously as if being followed. Her long blonde hair was suspended like silk down past her elbows. It blew playfully in the wind. She wore a teal silk gown which rustled in the leaves at her feet. Beside her walked a companion, slightly shorter with brunette hair falling in loose curls that contrasted brightly against her white and gold gown.

The blonde stepped out onto the street and looked around, seeking her location. The companion stayed on the street corner.

'Yvette,' the companion urged, her rosy cheeks flushed from the cold wind. 'You cannot walk these streets. If we are seen imagine what he will do?'

'Tatiana, my love,' whispered the blonde, turning to her companion, her voice gentle like a lullaby yet seductive as a minx. 'I do not fear Jareth. If this girl is the one, she will be more powerful than he, and she will return him back to his curse to live merely as the wings of the night.'

'What if she isn't the one?' Tatiana whispered, walking silently behind Yvette. 'She was raised mortal; she will not know our ways.'

'She is the daughter of Cassandra Atlanta. The power is a part of her. She will adjust and instinct will take over.'

Yvette stopped and turned to look at Tatiana, her face cast in shadows from the night sky. Tatiana, still uncertain of Yvette's faith, asked, 'And this child, what is her name?'

Yvette looked away for just a moment. When she looked back her green eyes held complete faith.

'Her name is Ariella Atlanta.'

CHAPTER TWO

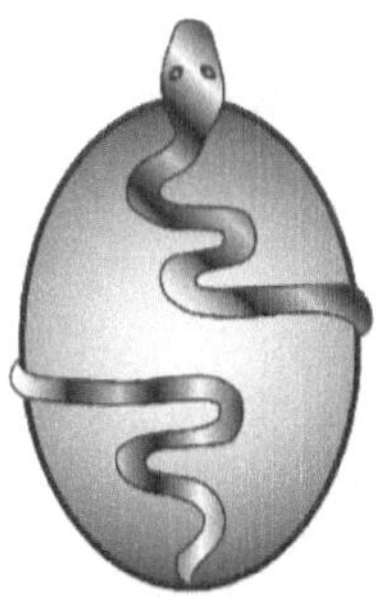

It started the same every night: I was standing in a rock pool beneath a waterfall, surrounded by trees. I wore a black silk night gown. I stared at my reflection which didn't match; in my reflection my night gown was white silk. Behind me, the sound of rushing water soothed the night air. Before me, standing amongst the trees was a man, staring at me, his face hidden within the shadows. I took a step forward to see his features but instead I fell beneath the water's surface, and a malicious laughter echoed above the surface.

'Ariella.'

The sound of someone calling me woke me from my sleep. I was gasping for breath. From downstairs I heard my aunt calling my name again and, as I did every morning, I silently thanked her for calling me from my dreams. I dragged myself out of bed and down the stairs to the kitchen.

'Tea, hon?' my Aunt asked me without turning around.

'Thanks Aurora,' I said as I sat down beside her current boyfriend, William. They'd been together for six months now, and that was a record for her. I thought he may be the one though, because they had been friends for as long as I could remember. He was a doctor, and he was decent looking...for an old guy. He wore crescent moon glasses and had thick, combed back hair. I was still waiting for the day to see him wearing something other than a suit.

'You over-slept again,' Aurora said as she sat at the table and handed me a mug of green tea.

'And? It's not like I am going to be late for school,' I said softly.

Aurora looked at me with her deep green eyes and I found myself wondering if we were actually related. Other than our mutual mocha skin we were complete opposites: she had straight brunette hair and I had black curls, and where she had deep green eyes I had ocean blue. I didn't see our similarities.

'I worry about you sweetheart,' Aurora said checking my temperature.

'So what do you want for your birthday, kiddo?' William asked.

I glanced over at him and shrugged. It would be my sixteenth birthday in a week and I hadn't planned anything; my birthday just never really excited me. I reached for the bowl of pitted cherries Aurora had put in the middle of the table; they were my absolute favourite.

'You don't want anything?' Aurora asked, sipping her tea.

'You could tell me about my parents.'

Aurora's mug hit the table so hard I was surprised it didn't break. 'You know the answer to that.'

I pushed back from the table and stormed up the stairs, slamming my door a little too dramatically. I went to my bedside table and pulled out a photo of my mum, and sat staring at the photo. We had the same blue eyes, but other than that she was identical to Aurora. The only thing I knew about her was her name, Cassandra. I wished I knew more. I didn't know anything about my father. I didn't understand why I couldn't know about them. I had the right.

For a moment I was mesmerised by the photo but shook myself out of it and put it back in the drawer. I glanced at the clock on my bedside table and realised I *was* going to be late for school. I went to my wardrobe and grabbed a black and cream, abstract-striped maxi-dress and a black belt. Walking into my bathroom I applied some eye make-up and brushed my hair back before leaving my room without a second glance in the mirror.

'Ariella,' Aurora called as I got my book bag from the lounge.

'What?' I snapped checking all my school books were in my bag and began to walk out the door.

CHAPTER THREE

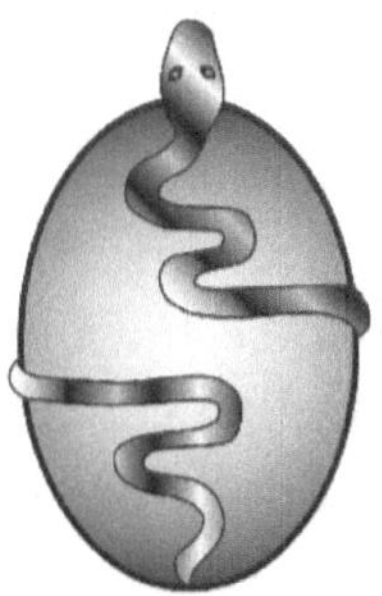

Waiting on the front lawn was my neighbour and best friend, Serena, who looked like an angel standing in the sun. Her long blond curls glowed like a halo, and she had legs that seemingly went on for miles.

'Wow. You're pissed,' Serena said as she started walking in step beside me to school.

'Don't ask,' I said as we continued to walk down the path and away from my house.

We lived in a small town called Mystic. It was surrounded by woods which brought horror movies to mind when I walked home at night.

From my bedroom window, beyond the trees, I could see mountains and I always wondered what lay behind them.

Being a small town there was only one high school, which consisted of less than two hundred students. As we entered the school grounds my friend Jordan ran up to us. He was all muscle, tanned with brown hair and hazel eyes you could just melt in.

'Where's the fire?' Serena asked, batting her lashes at Jordan.

'Jessica has Eva,' he said without taking his eyes off me.

I pushed passed Jordan and Serena and headed into the school. Jessica was the school bully who had a deep hatred of me and showed it by picking on little, rosy-cheeked Eva. Eva and I been friends since I saved her from Jessica on the first day of high school.

I was walking down the school corridor looking for Eva when I saw a crowd of people. As they saw me they moved aside, allowing me through.

Jessica's tall, slender figure was squeezed into a skin-tight black dress and she had Eva cornered against the lockers, talking in a voice too soft to hear. I pulled Jessica off Eva and pushed her into the lockers, holding her there.

'What's up Atlanta?' Jessica said as she attempted to squeeze out of my hold.

'I've had an extremely bad morning and don't want to deal with your a-hole attitude quite this early – now if you would, back off or you'll wish you never knew me.'

'I already wish that.'

After she spoke, a spark of electricity flew from me and zapped her. She jumped away.

'What did you just do?' she snapped.

I looked at her with no explanation.

'You're a freak,' she snarled before she stormed off. I watched as the crowd dispersed around me, looking over at Eva standing there with her strawberry blond curls and blue playsuit. Her brown eyes whispered a silent thanks.

'What happened this morning?' Eva asked as we walked to our English class.

'Just Aurora being stubborn,' I whispered as I played with a lock of my hair.

When I entered class I sat at my usual desk in the back corner and, like clockwork, Chantelle sat beside me and asked to borrow my homework. I handed her my notepad and pulled out my textbook. Eva never sat with us; she had her usual table in the front row, ready to learn. As I waited for my notepad I scribbled on my textbook absent-mindedly.

'That's cool. I didn't know you could draw,' Chantelle said as she handed me back my notepad.

I looked at her as if to ask her what she was talking about but then noticed my textbook, I had drawn the waterfall from my dream and a black cat-like symbol. I shut my textbook and dropped my pen, not trusting myself.

'Are you okay, Ariella?' Chantelle asked, looking at me with concern. 'You've been acting weird the past few weeks.'

I nodded. I'm not a very good liar. I had been acting differently because my dreams had become nightmares, and I was going insane trying to decipher them.

As I looked at Chantelle a chill ran down my spine; it sometimes unnerved me how much she looked like Jessica. I suppose, they were cousins. They had the same tall, slender bodies, dark mane of hair and green eyes. Their only major difference was clothes. Where Jessica's screamed "notice me", Chantelle dressed in chilled, punk-rocker style.

'Do you want to hang out after school?' Chantelle asked me as we left class. I knew she was only asking to make sure I was okay.

'I'm fine, plus I'm studying with your brother after school. I'll see you later,' I said, before disappearing into the crowd.

As I sat on the bleachers watching the boys play football I wondered what my friends would say if I told them what went on in my head. Would they have me committed to a mental institution?

'A single rose for a beauty with too many thoughts.'

I looked up to find myself staring into another set of green eyes, holding a rose. I smiled as I took the rose from Jay – his hair lighter than his sister's and his body all muscle – typical, handsome jock.

'What's on your mind?' he asked as he sat down beside me.

'Aurora and I had a fight because I want to know about my parents,' I said. 'I feel like this whole part of me is missing and if I don't know about my parents how will I ever know what that part is?'

Jay put his arm around me and looked at the ground. 'You don't need to know your parents to know who you are. Look at me, my parents are never around and I turned out fine.'

That's true. I had never met his parents and I had known Chantelle and Jay for years.

He gave me a kiss on the cheek and I cuddled into him.

'I have to go find my sister but I'll see you later,' he said before he got up and walked away.

CHAPTER FOUR

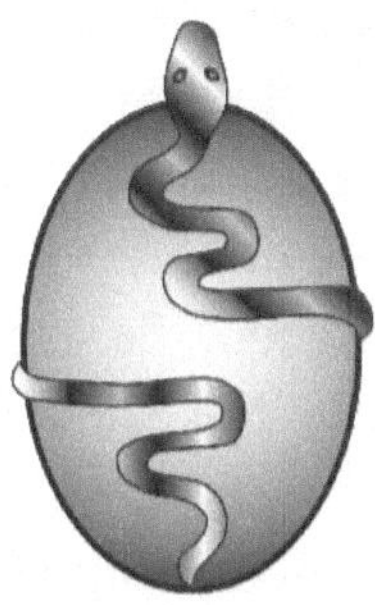

As I walked out of the school gate I found Serena and Eva waiting for me, both wearing a smile of mischief.

'What did you two do?' I asked as I reached them.

Eva handed me a shopping bag from behind her back. I eyed the bag suspiciously as I took it. I reached in and pulled out an amethyst purple shirt.

'You bought me a shirt?' I asked as I admired the material.

'It's a dress,' Serena said, rolling her eyes at me.

'Where's the rest of it?' I asked nervously.

Serena laughed. 'Stop stressing, you're going to look super hot.'

'We got you jewellery to go with it as well,' Eva squeaked excitedly.

'Thank you,' I said. 'But what is this for?'

'We are going to an underground party tonight,' Serena said enthusiastically.

'It's a school night,' I protested, while contemplating excuses I could come up with. 'Plus Aurora would never let me go.'

'I've already told Aurora that we have a school project tomorrow so you are staying over tonight.'

'You realise I live next door?' I asked. 'I can just go home when we're done.'

'Aurora said that too,' Serena said. 'I just said "you know how Ariella is, she'll probably doze off during study".'

'Hey!' I argued, though silently agreed. Serena may have thought of everything, but good luck to them getting me in that dress.

We got to Serena's house and I collapsed onto her bed. I was so exhausted. Her bedroom walls were plastered with photos of our group and other random memories. It also held a never ending supply of jewellery, make-up and shoes: a girl's heaven. Serena threw the dress at me, which I had hidden in my school bag, and begged me to at least try it on. I slipped into the so-called dress which was just longer than my fingertips and was tight enough to be a second skin. However, the shoulder straps added some class to it – a single strand of pearls.

'Now just sit down and close your eyes so I can work my magic,' Serena said as she steered me into the chair in front of the mirror.

I knew arguing was pointless so I sat down and closed my eyes. I felt the cold chain of the necklace she placed around my neck. I felt her remove my plain earrings and replace them with something heavier. I tried not to flinch as I felt her brushes move across my face. I prayed she'd keep it simple and didn't turn me into a drag queen.

'The masterpiece is complete,' Serena announced.

I opened my eyes to stare at my reflection. I was gorgeous! There were heavy black lines and purple shading around my eyes making them look huge, blood red lipstick and some kind of make-up making my cheeks look sharp and rosy. The jewellery I wore was silver with ruby red stones.

'Thank you!' I exclaimed.

'She appreciates your efforts,' Eva said emerging from the bathroom in a short blue dress and silver stilettos. 'That's a first.'

Serena handed me some red heels and then disappeared into the bathroom to decorate herself. I slipped my feet into the heels and then carefully walked over to the full length mirror. I had never been able to master heels and couldn't understand why girls wore them, but now I understood, my legs looked amazing.

Serena exited the bathroom in a skin-tight green dress and gold heels. As always she was the image of perfection.

Serena locked her door and put a movie on so if her step-monster walked past her room she wouldn't suspect anything. Her dad was always out of town on business and Serena had no interest in pleasing her new mother.

We each slipped off our high heels to climb out the window, throwing them out in front of us, onto the grass. I watched as Serena reached for a large branch outside her window, pulled herself onto it and navigated her way down the trunk to the ground. I followed, far less graceful, proving this wasn't Serena's first time climbing out her window this way, but definitely mine.

When I hit the ground I retrieved my heels and waited for Eva before we walked towards the party. I felt as though someone was watching me but resisted the urge to look back at my house just in case Aurora or the step-monster were staring out their windows.

As I walked in silence behind Serena and Eva, I wondered what I was getting myself into. I was not the party type. I heard the music before we turned the corner into the street. It was the first time I had seen this street so alive. It was always empty because only an abandoned church resided on it. The church was where the music and lights were coming from. I slipped back into my heels and we continued to walk towards the party. As I went up the stairs to enter the church I had a weird feeling that someone was watching me again. I turned around to look from the top of the stairs and found myself staring into a pool of people entering the party.

'Ariella,' Serena squeaked as she grabbed my hand. 'Let's go.'

Inside the church I found myself momentarily blinded by the strobe lights. It made me feel like everything was moving in slow motion. The music was so loud I thought my ear drums were about to explode. The high heels were starting to kill my feet.

'Let's get a drink,' Serena yelled over the music.

We pushed our way through the crowd, me holding onto Eva's hand and refusing to let go even as we reached the bar.

'Three Blue Furies,' I heard Serena yell to the bartender. My head whipped around to face her. Was she serious? Blue Furies were a mix of hallucinogen and alcohol. Someone started a rumour that it was bewitched by trickster fairies. Why this rumour actually caught on was beyond me. Fairies? Please!

'I can't do that,' I shouted to Serena as she put the shot in my hand.

'Sure you can,' she yelled back. 'Cheers.'

Eva and Serena raised their glasses, waiting for me. I looked at the blue liquid nervously. What the hell. I raised the glass before placing it to my lips and drank the whole thing in one gulp. I gasped, trying to breathe as it burned its way down my chest. I didn't know why people liked this stuff.

Serena grabbed my hands and dragged me onto the dance floor. As we danced to the music I felt my head begin to spin. I stumbled away from Serena and Eva. I needed fresh air and a moment to rest my feet.

I navigated my way through the sea of people to the front door. I reached the steps and sat down, my feet sighing in relief. As I sat there willing my head to stop spinning, a dark shadow approached me. I looked up and found myself speechless – the dark shadow was dangerously handsome.

'Are you okay?'

I nodded as he sat down beside me.

'How much have you had to drink?' he asked me.

'Just one,' I replied softly after finding my voice. 'It was just really smoky and I've never worn heels before tonight. I'm not really a party girl.'

I stole a glance at him and his dark, storm grey eyes met mine with a smile. I blushed.

'If you are ready to venture back inside, may I have this dance?' he asked as he stood up and offered me his hand.

I nodded, still blushing. I took his hand with a smile.

His grip felt warm against mine as he led me back inside and onto the dance floor. He spun me into him and put his hands on my hip, pulling me right into him. I put my arms around his neck and we moved to the music. He leaned down and kissed my neck and up to the corner of my mouth.

'Would you like a drink?' he asked, releasing me.

I nodded, worked up and speechless from what just happened, remembering the feel of his lips on my skin. I smiled. I almost had my first kiss.

Without warning a girl grabbed my chin and poured a glass of red liquid down my throat. I coughed and wiped my mouth. When I looked up she had already disappeared into the crowd. Whatever was in that glass intensified the spinning, the music got louder and the lights were now unbearably bright.

'Ariella,' I heard someone shout. 'Are you okay?'

I looked up and saw Serena. She grabbed my arm and walked me outside.

'How'd you hurt yourself?' Eva gasped once we were off the church steps.

I shook my head in confusion and then noticed the hand I'd wiped across my mouth. It was stained dark red.

'That looks like blood,' Serena said.

I had a sudden urge to be sick. What kind of person would make someone drink blood?

'We'd better get going or we won't wake up for school tomorrow,' Eva said.

CHAPTER FIVE

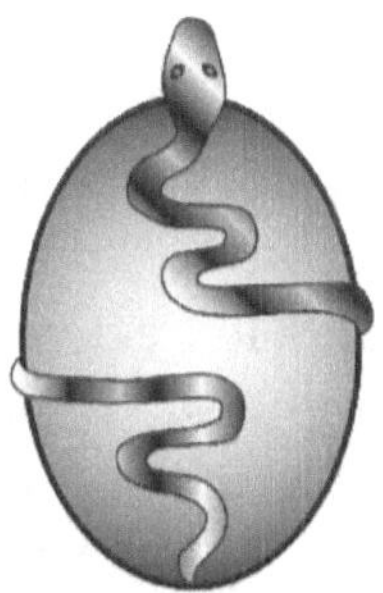

As we walked home the memory of the girl pouring blood down my throat replayed in my mind. Blood. Urgh. What was I talking about? It wouldn't have been blood. It was just some red alcohol.

'Are you okay?' Eva asked me.

'Just cold,' I lied.

Oh god!

I just left the party, he said he was getting us drinks and I just left. I felt so horrible. I finally met a nice guy and I ditched him. I didn't even know his name.

We reached Serena's house and watched her climb the tree and go back through her window. Eva and I waited for her to come down and unlock the back door. The moment Serena unlocked the door I ran upstairs to the bathroom and washed my mouth out and the red stain off my hand.

I found some make-up wipes in the draw and started erasing Serena's artwork until my canvas was once again clear. Serena had a double bed and a couch in her room. I volunteered for the couch since I still didn't know if my dreams caused me to stir. I rearranged the pillows and curled up underneath the blanket.

Serena told us about the boys she danced with as she removed her make-up and jewellery. Eva slipped into bed and fell asleep straight away. I contemplated telling Serena about the boy I met but then she would ask for every last detail and yell at me for leaving without his name so I kept my mouth shut.

As I fell asleep and into my dream, I felt that it would be different tonight. I wasn't standing on the cliffs as usual, I was standing in a glass box, the room outside was pure darkness. I felt water at my feet. I looked down and saw the water was actually blood. A scream rose in my throat. I began to panic. I banged my fist on the glass as hard as I could. That's when I saw him, the guy from the party. He walked up to the glass box and laughed at me. I screamed for him to help me but he disappeared into the darkness. The blood was now up to my neck. Something pulled me under and the blood entered my mouth. I started to choke and woke up gasping for air.

Serena and Eva were still fast asleep but my heart was pounding. I knew I wouldn't get back to sleep. I was still awake as the sun came up. I watched the colours bleed into each other. It was one of the true beauties in the world.

Serena's alarm broke my concentration and I stretched out over the couch. Eventually we all got ready for school in silence, all exhausted from the lack of sleep. Eva handed me a bottle of water which I downed in seconds. I hadn't realised how parched I was. I also felt a mild ache residing in the back of my head; an easy first hangover, though my feet were numb and sore.

I grabbed an apple from the fruit bowl downstairs as we dragged ourselves out the back door. We reached the school fence when a strange feeling washed over me. I watched Serena wander off with Jay and Eva walking in the direction of her locker. But I stood frozen at the gate.

Without fully knowing or understanding what I was doing I turned around and walked off to the park. I smiled as I reached my destination and saw him waiting for me. I walked over to him and wondered what I would say for ditching him at the party last night.

'Hi,' he said before I could get anything out.

'I'm sorry,' I blurted out, 'for leaving last night without saying goodbye.'

He put his hand to my cheek and his touch felt warm.

'I'm just sorry I didn't get to do this,' he whispered as he leaned into me. 'I was thinking about it all night,' he said as his lips were just before mine.

I closed my eyes, ready for my first kiss.

I suddenly gasped in pain as something sharp was jammed into my stomach. I opened my eyes and found a knife sticking out of my abdomen. I was completely alone. I pulled the knife out before I collapsed.

A light flickered across my vision as I woke up. I opened my eyes to see William standing over me reading a chart, and Aurora asleep in a chair beside me.

'What happened?' I groaned.

William put his hand to my head in a soothing fatherly gesture.

'You were found unconscious in a park, covered in blood, but not a cut on you.'

Did I hallucinate the knife?

'But,' he continued, 'weird thing was, it was your blood.'

He put down the chart he was reading. 'Medically we have no idea what happened.'

'What do you mean medically?'

He smiled at me then turned to leave the room.

When he got to the door I called out, 'William…what is wrong with me?'

He came back over to me and tucked a strand of hair behind my ear.

'Nothing sweetheart. Get some rest. I'm sure Aurora will explain everything to you.'

What did he mean? He turned and left before I could ask. What would he and Aurora know?

I looked over at Aurora who was now awake. She stood up and sat on the edge of my bed.

'What happened sweetheart?' she asked, her eyes red and puffy like she had been crying.

'I skipped school,' I said.

'I know,' she replied as she stroked my cheek. 'But why did you do that? First you sneak out and go to a party with Serena and then you skip school. It's not like you?'

'How do you know about the party?' I argued.

'I'm not stupid; I saw you girls climbing out Serena's window.'

'You're spying on me now?' I yelled, unsure of why I was the one getting angry.

Aurora sighed then walked out of the room, closing the door behind her. I watched as William approached her and they started talking in hushed whispers.

I climbed out of bed and walked over to the door, pressing my ear to it to eaves drop on their conversation.

'I don't know what has gotten into her the last few months. Her aura is having darkness creep into it and I hear her talking in her sleep. I don't know what to do to protect her.'

'How long did you sleep?' I heard William ask her.

'A few hours maybe? I am surprised I can even close my eyes.'

'Do you know what happened?' he asked.

'I have no idea. None of our line has healing powers. Cassandra and I never did.'

Powers?

The doctor came and I got back to the bed. He had come to take a blood sample but he looked only a few years older than me.

'Are you doing my test?' I asked as he put the needle in the vein in my arm.

He smiled politely at me. 'Yes I am, Miss Atlanta'

'Can you tell me why I fainted and had my blood on me?'

'I was hoping you would tell me,' he said as he took the needle out.

'If I tell you something you have to keep it secret because of doctor patient confidentiality right?'

He walked to the end of my bed and picked up my chart. 'Yes. Does this mean you do not wish your other doctors to know?'

'No, I don't want William to know,' I said with guilt.

He put the chart back. 'Tell me your story then.'

I looked at the door to make sure Aurora wasn't still outside the room. 'I think I was drugged,' I said as I looked back at the doctor. 'I went to a party and some girl forced this drink down my throat and everything got loud and bright and I kept spinning and I still didn't feel myself when I woke up this morning.'

He pulled a small jar out of his jacket. 'It's for a urine sample, and I'll send it to the lab when I send down your blood work.'

Awkwardly I took the urine jar and walked into the bathroom.

When I emerged from the bathroom I saw Aurora was back sitting in her chair. The doctor took my urine sample and left the room.

'What do you need a urine sample for?' Aurora asked me as I climbed back into the bed.

'He's just doing heaps of test to try and explain what happened to me,' I said without meeting her eyes.

It had been a few hours since I had overheard Aurora and William's conversation but I was now at home and comfy in my own bed.

'How are you feeling honey?' Aurora asked as she sat on the side of my bed.

'Fine,' I murmured.

'What happened sweetheart?' she asked me softly.

'I don't know,' I lied. 'I can't remember. I just want to sleep, I'm tired.'

She nodded and walked out.

I woke before sunrise and decided to get ready for school. Another day in bed would drive me crazy.

Aurora was putting the kettle on for tea as I walked into the kitchen.

'What are you doing up sweetheart?' Aurora asked as I sat down.

'I'm going to school,' I said as though she had forgotten.

'But you're still recovering from...'

'From what?' I snapped, interrupting her.

Aurora looked away from me. 'I want you to come home straight from school today.'

'Fine,' I said harshly as I pushed away from the table. Serena must have thought I was staying home today too. She wasn't waiting for me so I walked to school alone.

CHAPTER SIX

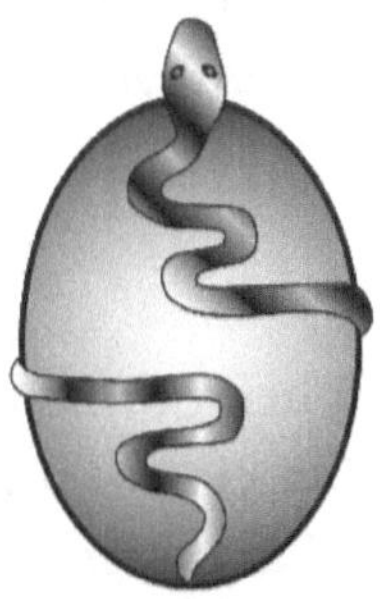

'Hey Ariella,' I heard Jay say before he fell into step with me. 'What happened to you? I got told you were in hospital, no visitors allowed and no one would tell us anything.'

'I don't know what happened,' I said. 'I guess I fainted and woke up in a hospital.'

I reached my English class and walked to my usual seat, where I sat and stared out the window. I felt as though I was standing beneath the waterfall from my dream, the water running through my fingers. I saw a girl with shadows hiding her face standing before me, handing me a glass of red liquid. She whispered, 'protection'.

Protection from what? I wondered.

She tapped her finger to her temple. 'I can hear your thoughts,' she said with a smile.

I looked at the glass she handed me.

'Drink,' she said. 'It saves you from harm, heals all wounds…knife wounds.'

'You know about the knife wound?' I asked with my mind.

She nodded, her eyes stood out from the shadows but I couldn't see any of her other features. 'He wants to kill you; you are a threat to him.'

'Who is he?'

'He is family.'

A book dropped behind me making me jump; everyone was leaving class. I'd zoned out for the whole hour. I looked at the desk beside me where Chantelle sat but she was already gone. I wondered why she didn't ask to borrow my homework. I gathered my books and quickly left the classroom with everyone else.

The lunch bell rang and I saw Serena, Jay and Eva all sitting on the oval laughing, and something churned inside of me, a feeling of unease. Before they saw me, I disappeared to the other side of the school and sat at one of the empty tables to work on an assignment that I had been neglecting.

'Why are you hiding?' asked a familiar voice.

I looked up as Jordan slid into the seat beside me. I shook my head.

'What's up princess?' he asked me casually.

I smiled at the nickname he used when he noticed my bad moods.

'I feel like I am going crazy,' I said more to myself than to him.

'Want my opinion?' he asked.

'You'll give it to me anyway,' I mused.

He laughed softly. 'I think you're amazing, and if you ever need help I will be the first man by your side. Because for one you're the only girl that doesn't throw herself at me, and two I love you and I'll never admit saying that if you tell anyone.'

I leaned over and hugged him, afraid I'd cry if I said anything back.

The school day was finally over, and I knew I was meant to go straight home from school but I wandered to the park. It wasn't a fancy park or filled with rides for screaming kids, it was just a small oval with some trees and a few wooden benches. I laid beneath my favourite tree holding my book to my chest. I closed my eyes for just a minute, but fell into a dream.

This time the dream was different again. I was falling. I wanted to scream, but before I could, I hit the ground. I was in an empty room built of stone. The only decoration was a red curtain. I pushed it aside and stepped through the doorway, finding myself in a rainforest of vibrant colours. As I went to step forward, a loud roar echoed through the forest making the ground beneath my feet vibrate. And then I woke from the dream.

I sat up and placed my face in my hands, ran my hands back through my hair and looked around the park. It was still as empty as it was before I fell asleep. I rolled onto my stomach and opened my book. The story was about a girl that lived on a farm and the boy that helps her out always answers her with 'As you wish.'

I suddenly heard a voice so I looked up from my book to see two women walking through the park. I glanced at them from underneath my eyelashes. The woman with the teal dress and blonde hair looked annoyed at her brunette friend who was speaking. I kept my eyes on them but I was too far to away to hear their conversation. They both turned around to look at me so I quickly turned away pretending to be interested in my book.

I heard a rustling of leaves and then a soft voice. 'Are you Ariella Atlanta?'

I looked up and the two women had both walked over to me. I got to my feet and stood before them.

'Yes, and you are?' I asked, hiding my nerves over them knowing my identity.

'Oh of course, how rude of me, I am Yvette and this is my companion, Tatiana,' said the blonde.

'How do you know me?'

Yvette hesitated, as if looking for the right words while Tatiana glanced at her nervously.

'We knew your mother.'

For a moment I fell silent. Could this be real?

'But…how?' I whispered, after I found my voice.

'We used to follow her, she was a great leader,' Tatiana whispered, as though remembering. She snapped out of the memory and asked, 'Do you have unexplainable dreams?'

I nodded.

'That's good, it means your lock is fading,' Yvette said before turning serious. 'Have you ever walked past the white mansion on Everson Road?'

'What do you mean by lock?' I asked.

'The lock on your memory,' Yvette said as though that explained it.

'But how is there a lock on my mind. You can't just lock a mind; it doesn't make sense.'

'It's a magic lock,' Tatiana explained. 'It was put on your mind when you first moved here.'

'But magic doesn't exist.'

'We are getting off track here,' Yvette cut in. 'Have you ever seen the white mansion on Everson Road?'

'Aurora has forbidden me to walk down the road,' I said, now wondering why I ever paid attention to that stupid rule.

'The person who lives there…' Yvette paused, as though she didn't know how to continue. 'He is in possession of a locket that has the potential to destroy humanity.'

'A locket has the potential to destroy humanity?' I asked.

'Yes,' she said without hesitation. 'No one is sure how to work it, but we know it's dangerous and we need to get hold of it so we can keep it from ever being activated.'

I laughed, unable to resist. They looked at me in shock.

'I'm sorry but what you're saying is crazy.'

'We are telling you the truth. This isn't a story,' Tatiana said with a serious look on her face.

I stopped laughing. 'Oh, you're being serious? But why are you telling me?'

'Because your mother was the most powerful witch ever known,' Tatiana said.

'Until you,' Yvette inserted quickly. 'When you come of age you will be able to access that power. When Aurora took you in, she did a binding spell so you couldn't use magic until you were sixteen and if our sources are correct that is in a few days.'

'You're talking crazy!' I exclaimed. 'My mother wasn't a witch, and neither am I – magic does not exist.'

Tatiana took a step towards me. She bent down and picked up a small pebble from the grass. She placed it in her palm and looked at me. 'Just watch the pebble okay?' she said before she looked down at her hand.

I rolled my eyes but looked at the pebble in her hand anyway. At first nothing happened, but then the pebble started to rise from her hand. It rose up to my eye level. I took a step back from Tatiana.

'How did you do that?' I asked, panic flooding my voice.

'I am a witch, just like your mother and just like you,' she said as the pebble floated back down into her palm.

'Now that you've seen magic exists you can do this,' Yvette said, stepping up beside Tatiana. 'You are the only one who can do it. No one else can steal it'

'Steal?' I exclaimed a little too loudly.

Yvette took my hand in hers and looked into my eyes. 'The locket is called the Talen'i'palurin – and only an heir of Aubrey can steal it.'

'Aubrey, as in my father?'

CHAPTER SEVEN

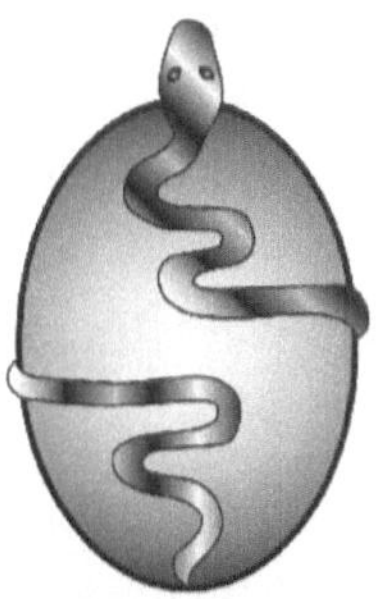

It was just a dream. I just have to pinch myself and I'll wake up. I pinched my arm as hard as I could but I was still just walking home from the park. I looked back at where the strange conversation had taken place. Yvette and Tatiana were gone. I was so confused; I didn't understand anything that just happened. I needed to talk to someone. But who? I didn't really know how to explain this to any of my friends. Aurora, she would know. I'd just ask her.

Once I got home I was suddenly too nervous to say anything, I sat in silence at the already set dinner table.

'And who is that lovely guest I ran into upstairs?' William asked as he and Aurora sat down to eat.

What guest? I wondered.

'That's Arya,' Aurora said. 'She is the daughter of an old friend of mine. She's just staying here a few days. I only found out myself last night.'

'An old friend?' he enquired. 'She has very similar features to Ariella. I thought for a moment that she might be another family member. Is she not joining us?'

Aurora looked over at William with a soft smile, which I could see was full of love. 'No darling. She's had a long day travelling and just wanted to sleep.'

'How was your day Ariella?' Aurora asked.

'We have a guest that looks like me?' I asked, ignoring her question.

'Similar to you,' William said. 'Like she could almost be your sister.'

William smiled at Aurora and they both returned to their meals. I looked back and forth between them. How did I not know we had a guest?

The three of us ate in silence. I was itching to say something but it was not something I could just blurt out in front of William.

I wish I was telepathic so I could talk to Aurora, I thought to myself.

'What?'

I looked up and Aurora was looking at me weirdly.

'Sweetheart, what is it?' William asked placing his hand on hers.

'Nothing,' she said looking away from me. 'I just thought I heard something.'

What just happened? I was so confused. *Did she just hear my thoughts?* I tried to think of nothing and let me tell you that it was harder than you think. We finished eating in silence, then William cleared the plates and left the room, leaving Aurora and I alone.

'You heard my thoughts,' I blurted out.

'Don't be stupid Ariella,' she said as she went to leave the table.

'What's the Talen'i'palurin?' I asked.

Aurora sat back down and looked at me nervously. 'Where did you hear that?'

I didn't say anything. Aurora glanced around to ensure William wasn't within hearing range. 'What do you know?' she asked.

'That I am an heir of Aubrey.'

Aurora came over and knelt before me, taking my hand in hers. 'Listen to me Ariella, whatever anyone asks you to do, don't do it.'

I looked away from her; she brushed her fingers through my hair.

'Sweetheart,' she whispered, her voice breaking slightly. 'Your mother wouldn't want you to relive her mistakes.'

'What?' I exclaimed, snatching my hand back and standing up. 'My mother tried to steal it?'

'Yes, but only those of his bloodline can take it without being driven insane.'

'Are you telling me my mother went insane?'

Aurora sighed. I could see the mental battle waging in her mind; she had kept this from me for so long.

'No, your father killed her.'

'My father?' I cried. 'For all these years, I've been asking about my parents and you've told me nothing. Not a single thing. Now you just blurt out that my father killed my mother! I cried over not knowing him.'

'I was trying to protect you,' Aurora said sadly.

'Well you did a fantastic job of that,' I snapped.

'Ariella,' Aurora sighed.

I took a step back from Aurora, feeling as though I was falling into oblivion. Without another word, I ran up to my room and slammed my door behind me.

'He is still alive you know,' said a voice I didn't recognise.

I looked up and standing in my bathroom doorway was a girl not much older than me. She had olive skin, which was still damp from her shower; she stood before me in nothing but a towel, casually drying her long, black hair with another towel.

'I'm Arya. The guest bathroom doesn't have hot water.'

'You look familiar,' I questioned.

'I should,' she scoffed. 'I saved your life.'

I gave her a vacant expression hoping she would elaborate.

She sighed. 'I poured the blood down your throat at that hormonal dance you attended.'

'That was you?' I exclaimed. 'What kind of freak pours blood down someone's throat?'

'If I didn't you would have bled to death in that park,' she said bluntly. 'My blood, it has healing powers,' she added with a shrug.

It was all too much to wrap my head around.

'Wait,' I said. 'If you knew, why didn't you prevent him from hurting me?'

'Killing you darling,' she said sarcastically. 'And I didn't know what he was going to do. I was being proactive.'

'Proactive?' I repeated, my voice laced with sarcasm and annoyance. 'You poured blood down my throat because you were being proactive.'

'Listen,' she snapped, dropping the towel that was drying her hair. 'He tried to kill you, possibly on your father's orders, so don't get touchy with me.'

I didn't say anything back. Was it possible my father wanted to kill me? I went to turn away when

Arya spoke again. 'If you didn't hear me before, he's still alive.'

'What do you mean he is still alive?' I asked.

'Your father – don't ask where he is though. He has been vacant from Alesmera for the past few years – that's your birth home – he has a son though, Jareth. He is your brother in case you didn't know. Not the biggest fan of me, so don't mention my name if you see him.'

'How do you know all this?' I asked. 'I don't even know you.'

'I'm here for a few days, I might tell you,' she said before she walked past me and out of my room.

CHAPTER EIGHT

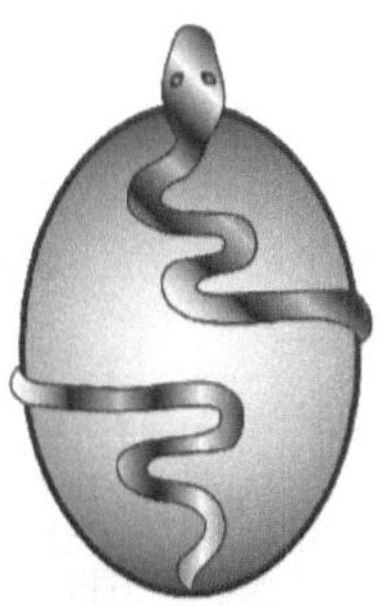

It was impossible to sleep after all the events of the day. That didn't mean I wasn't trying when the doorbell rang. I looked at the clock on my bedside table. It was flashing ten past eleven; it was way too late for a social call. I snuck out of my room and sat on the step that gave me both the best view and eavesdropping position to the kitchen. Aurora had her back to whoever was speaking.

'We have to tell her the truth,' said the visitor, now stepping into view. Yvette. 'She is the daughter of Cassandra, the true heir to the throne and the only one with the power to defeat Jareth.'

Aurora slammed her mug on the bench and turned to face Yvette. 'You had no right to tell her. Cassandra died to keep her out of this life. I respected my sister's wish by raising her daughter as a mortal – I stripped her powers as well as mine to avoid temptation and suspicion.'

'She died trying to keep the locket out of her husband's hands,' Yvette argued. 'And what are you going to do when she turns sixteen? Her powers will reactivate and then he will sense her, find her, and kill her.'

Aurora slapped Yvette so hard that I jumped at the sound.

'He will not hurt her. I will not repeat history. I will keep her inactive.'

Yvette's hand rested on her cheek, her face in shock. 'Why do you have such little faith in her?'

Aurora looked hurt and shocked at the accusation.

'We have risked much in coming here. If Jareth knew we had crossed the border he'd have Tatiana and I killed, but we took the risk because I have faith that Ariella will succeed,' Yvette whispered as she placed what looked like a locket on the table.

Aurora picked up the locket and opened it. Her face turned sad as she placed her hand on her heart. 'If Ariella goes down this path she will learn things that would destroy her.' She dropped the locket back onto the table.

Yvette cleared her throat. 'If Jareth wins, he will take control of not just Alesmera but everywhere. I shudder to imagine what he would do to the mundane folk.'

'I forbid you to tell her anymore. Fight Jareth on your own. He is just a child himself. He can't be too difficult to take,' Aurora fumed.

'You know who his father is!' Yvette growled. 'If Aubrey trained him from birth, who knows what powers we can expect him to have.'

'That is my point exactly,' Aurora snapped, her face blushing from anger. 'If you can't defeat him how do you expect Ariella to?'

'The child born from darkness and light will possess the strength from both worlds, making them the most powerful hybrid known in Alesmera,' Yvette recited from memory. 'Is it right to sacrifice the world for one child?'

'Get. Out. Now,' Aurora said dangerously.

'You know there are people sleeping upstairs right?' said Arya as she walked into the kitchen. I didn't even see where she came from. Yvette looked at her in shock, as if she had seen a ghost. 'Don't looked so surprised to see me; you're making me feel unwelcome.'

'I need. . .' Yvette stutters, struggling to find the words. 'Aurora needs to tell Ariella the truth, about everything.'

'Why are you obsessed with getting the locket from him?' Arya asked as she sat down.

Yvette looked at Arya, first with shock and then with rage. 'Are you accusing me of...'

'Yes,' Arya interrupted, unfazed with the tension rising. 'He's had the locket for years. He doesn't know how to use it. The big mystery is who does? Who is going to bring through the world's end?'

'How do we know it's not you?' Yvette snarled.

Arya looked at her darkly. She glanced over at Aurora who was still fuming, sighed and remained calm. 'I believe Aurora asked you to leave.'

Yvette spun on her heel and walked out the front door leaving behind a fuming Aurora. Aurora ran her hands through her hair and walked into the lounge room where she collapsed onto the couch. Arya walked up the stairs and winked at me as she passed. I waited until I heard her door close. As silent as a mouse, I slipped into the kitchen and stole the locket from the table. I opened it and saw two photos: one of my mum and a man, the other of a baby. Me.

CHAPTER NINE

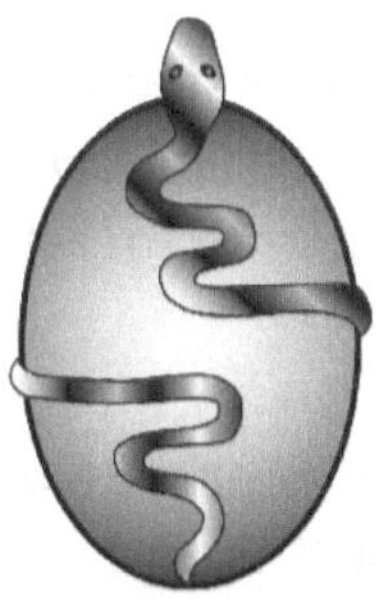

As Serena and I walked to school the following day, I couldn't get Aurora and Yvette's conversation out of my head. The silver locket I stole from the table was now cold against my skin, hiding under my dress.

'You're coming to dinner tonight at Jordan's right?' Serena asked as we walked into the school grounds. 'His parents are out of town.'

I nodded and smiled in response. I walked down the hall to my locker and found Jessica leaning against it, blocking my access.

'Hello princess,' she said venomously. 'Where is your pet mouse? Is she is hiding from me today?'

'Move,' I commanded, and without even touching her, she was thrown to the floor. Before I had time to freak out she stood back up and smirked at me.

'The gloves are off today kitty cat,' she said, pushing me into the lockers.

I tried to remain calm.

'Come on Atlanta. Why such the good girl?' Jessica said as she pushed me again.

'Back off,' I said harshly, throwing her back into the lockers on the other side of the hall. I looked at her with shock and disappeared down the hall. I didn't stop running until I reached the park – my lungs burning.

Everson Road.

I just kept repeating those words, a panic attack rising in my chest. I pulled the locket out from under my dress and looked at the photo of my parents. *They looked so happy. Why did he betray her?* I just wanted to throw the locket in a fit of rage but part of me couldn't let it go.

Everson Road, I said to myself again.

That wasn't far from here. Before I realised what I was doing I was walking to the street where I was forbidden to go. I walked down the footpath to the house I had only heard about. As I stood across the street, I was awestruck at the cold feeling the house washed over me. It was a large, stone and marble mansion with enormous, black steel gates. Without warning, my lungs got heavy and I found it hard to breathe. A pain burst within my chest and before I could run, I collapsed and fell into darkness.

I found myself standing in a nursery. Its pale blue walls were covered in glow-in-the-dark stars. In the corner, a woman in a white dress with sapphire blue eyes was smiling down at a baby in her arms. Could it be…I called out *Mum*, but she didn't turn around. I walked up to the woman and stood before her. It was her, the same as in my photo. I leaned in to hug her but fell through her. It was as if I was not there. I went and stood next to her and realised the baby must be me. But it couldn't be. The baby had grey eyes, not blue.

I walked out the nursery door and found myself standing on a cliff in a violent storm. I tried to turn around to go back into the room but it had disappeared. I wiped the rain from my face and saw that my hands were red. The sky was raining blood. I took a step back and fell off the cliff. As I screamed, a cold, malevolent laugh encircled me.

I landed in a lake and swum to the surface finding myself, once again, in the waterfall that's haunted my dreams the past few months. Looking into the trees, I found the man who was always watching me. I screamed at him to reveal himself but a cold laugh just filled the air again.

I woke up.

The images I had seen or the blackout should have been what made me panic in the moment, but no. It was the fact that I woke up back in the park.

I reached for my bag and pulled out a watch that I always kept in it. School finished three hours ago. I was meant to be at Jordan's. It also meant that I was unconscious for over eight hours. I quickly brushed myself off and got to my feet before I started to run all the way to Jordan's house.

I was holding my ribs and gasping for air when Jay answered the door.

'Ariella,' he said, sounding shocked. 'Thank you for finally gracing us with your presence, but what the hell happened to you today?'

'Jessica got to me. I needed to clear my head,' I said, not making eye contact.

'Well come on in. It's bad luck to linger in doorways or so you've taught me,' he said ushering me in.

As I entered, I saw the others spread out over Jordan's couches. I went over and sat down beside Serena. Eva was so excited about my confrontation with Jessica.

'I can't believe you did what you did. You should have seen Jessica later in the day; she was all brooding,' Eva exclaimed.

I stopped paying attention, my mind elsewhere, thinking about the locket and the images I had seen.

'Ariella?'

'What?' I said, startled, bringing myself back to reality.

'Are you okay?' Eva asked, looking concerned.

With an exhausted sigh, I ran my hand over my face. 'It's stupid; you'll have me admitted to a mental institution if I tell you.'

'Babe, you can tell us anything. Jordan often tells us way too much,' Serena said with a gentle smile. That made me laugh. Jordan looked mildly offended but shrugged because he knew it was true.

'Okay,' I said with a deep breath. I sat up straight. 'You know how I don't know much about my parents? Well, I met these two women who knew them and they told me something crazy, like imagination gone wild.'

'What did they say?' Eva asked sitting forward.

'That…' I took a deep, nervous breath, 'my half-brother has this necklace that can destroy the world and my mother was attempting to steal it and that when I turn sixteen my brother will be able to sense me because I have magic and it was my destiny to steal the necklace.' I spoke really fast and refused to look up.

'That's…different,' Jordan said slowly after what felt like hours.

'What can we do to help?' Eva said. 'We need to plan a mission. Where is the locket?'

I looked up at her expecting her expression to hold mockery but instead I found she was serious, no laughter.

'We should do the heist in the next few days,' Jay said as Serena pulled out her laptop.

I looked at him in complete and utter shock.

'We can organise a plan, but we should do it before your birthday so he doesn't sense you. Where is the locket?' Serena asked whilst she typed away on her laptop. I told her all I knew and she disappeared into her electronic world.

I felt as though I may be hallucinating. Were they really being this supportive? Perhaps they were planning to admit me to a mental institution, or I was just being crazy and I have amazing friends. 'What if you guys get hurt or something?' I asked my fear out loud.

'We will be fine, promise,' Chantelle said with an honest smile.

'You don't understand,' I argue. 'These two women were too scared to face him, but are expecting me to face him.'

'Ariella,' Serena said, forcing my attention on her. 'I know you didn't ask for this, but it's been given to you. You can't just sit on this information and do nothing.'

'Let's start planning then,' I said with a forced smile. While everyone gathered around Serena pitching their ideas, I got up and walked outside to sit on the front stairs. Eva came and sat beside me.

'What are you feeling?' Eva asked.

'I just wish my whole life didn't feel like a lie. I mean I wonder what would have happened if Aurora got her way to keep me inactive and I didn't find out. He could have found me one day and killed me and I wouldn't have had a fighting chance.'

Serena, followed by the others, joined us on the porch.

'I have blueprints of the house. I just need some more time to polish the plan so let's meet at 3am tomorrow. Sound good?' Serena asked.

'I'm impressed, this should be your mission instead of mine,' I said softly.

CHAPTER TEN

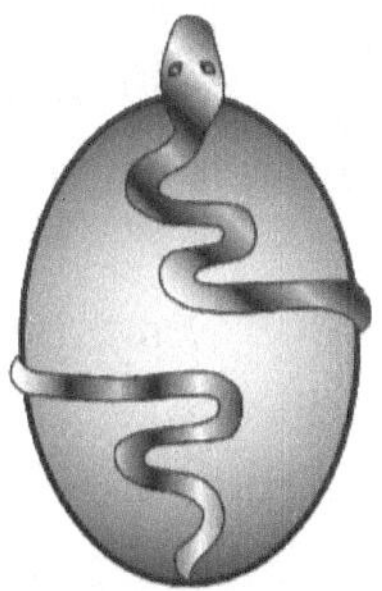

It was late when I got home from Jordan's house. I slipped through the front door as silently as possible and took tiny steps towards the staircase. As I walked past the lounge room, a voice broke the silence.

'You're troubled,' said a familiar voice from the lounge room. 'I can sense it. You need to learn to hide your emotions.'

I walked into the lounge room and found the towel girl, Arya, sitting by the window with her nose in a book.

'How do you do that?' I asked.

She doesn't look up, but said, 'Self-control.'

I rolled my eyes and went to walk away when she said, 'It won't work by the way. Mortals know nothing of our world.'

I sat down before her. 'You don't know that,' I replied with as much confidence as I could.

Finally, her eyes left the book and met mine. 'Perhaps. But just because your friend can search information on the internet, it doesn't make her an expert. She doesn't know anything about magic. She won't be able to find the magical protections that are around that house. But you can. You'll be able to feel the magic's print. It'll take you a while to learn how to read the prints, but if you sense it, find a different way.'

I wanted to question what she meant but before I could find the words, she held her hand out to me with a smile playing upon her lips. I felt compelled and my hands embraced hers. Immediately I felt a surge of electricity pulse through my veins. I looked into her eyes and realised they matched mine. Above us the night sky echoed with thunder.

I snatched my hand away. 'What was that?'

She looked at me with yearning and darkness. 'A taste of your powers,' she whispered. 'Better sneak up to your room. Aurora just woke up, and Ariella, my bet's on the number three,' she said as she returned to her book.

Without another word to Arya, I left the lounge and snuck up to my room. I didn't even bother changing, but just collapsed onto my bed. I lay there restless, sleep unable to find me, my mind reeling over what was able to happen. I finally dozed off and a dream began.

I was in a throne room. Before me sat an occupied throne. The man seemed familiar but his face was covered in shadows. Drawn to his power I walked forward when Arya emerged wearing a blue and silver gown. It was nothing like the girl I'd seen in my house. 'Beware the mission. Among friends lie enemies.'

She turned away and walked through a mirror. It rippled like water. It stilled and I walked to it and stood before it. I saw myself, in a black dress with a sword by my side. I looked down and I was wearing a white dress, confused I looked up again. This time my reflection stepped out of the mirror and swung the sword at me. I defensively threw my hand up and the blade slashed my palm. I screamed in pain.

I woke up and held a second scream when I saw that my hand was actually bleeding. I heard my doorknob turn and hid my hand under my sheet, fearing Aurora's reaction. I let out a sigh of relief when I saw it was Arya. She closed the door behind her.

'Show me your hand,' she said as she walked over to the bed.

'How'd you know?' I asked as she sat on the edge. I held out my hand.

She ignored my question and asked, 'In the dream were you the white or the black?'

'White,' I whispered. 'What does that mean?'

She examined my hand as she spoke. 'It means your mum's genes are dominant, which is a good thing.'

She released my hand and pulled out a small knife from her back pocket. She sliced it across her palm and quickly grabbed my hand so her blood mixed with mine.

'Isn't this how diseases are transferred?' I asked nervously.

'With the magic in our blood it's impossible for us to get a mortal disease. When was the last time you were ever sick?' she asked as she released my hand.

I watched with fascination as the wound closed up.

'Good luck with your heist,' Arya said, then stood up and left my room.

CHAPTER ELEVEN

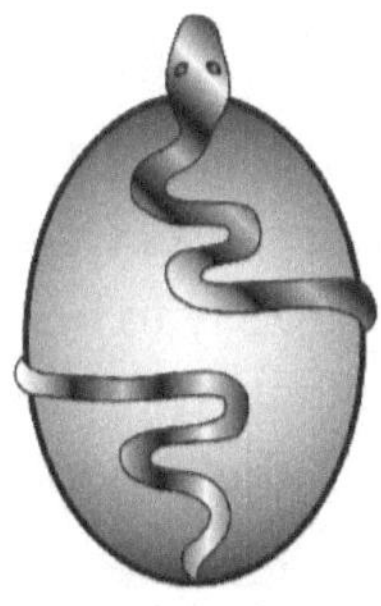

It was here.

Today was the day. Tonight I would be breaking and entering, then stealing to save the world. I felt like there were butterflies raging a war in my stomach. I would be amazed if we managed to pull this off. Heading downstairs to the breakfast table, I found Arya in a conversation with Aurora. I caught the words Alesmera and Jareth.

'What about Jareth?' I asked as I sat down. Aurora looks as though she was seeking a change of subject.

'I was just telling your Aunt about how the last time I was with your brother I left him in handcuffs,' Arya said laughing at the memory, unaware of the tension.

'I want to see Alesmera,' I whispered.

Aurora went rigid. 'You are forbidden,' she said with a dangerous growl.

I glanced at Arya who was staring down at her cup with a knowing smile playing upon her lips.

Aurora and Arya fell back into conversation so I excused myself from the table and fetched my bag to leave for school.

Serena, as usual, was waiting for me when I walked out of the house. As we walked to school, I found I had nothing to say to her. My head was too wrapped up in what we planned to attempt tonight. We entered the school grounds and Jay walked up to us, saying he was on his way to the library. I watched him and Serena walk off and I wandered to my locker alone.

'Why do we fight?' asked an all too familiar voice as I closed my locker.

I looked over at Jessica who was leaning against the locker beside mine.

'We'd make an awesome team if we join forces,' she said with the same knowing smile that I saw on Arya this morning. I felt as though I was missing something.

'I'll never join you,' I said harshly, then walked off to my first class.

I entered the classroom and placed my notebook on the table beside me for Chantelle, knowing she'd want to copy my homework. I opened my textbook not really reading the words. I heard the teacher talking but I continued attempting to read the textbook while I drowned in my own thoughts.

The bell rang, breaking me from my thoughts.

Chantelle handed me back my notebook, and said, 'Serena said we have to meet her on the oval.'

I gathered my books and followed Chantelle out of the classroom and down onto the oval. There was no sport training today so we were alone. It was eerily quiet out there.

'Now here is the plan,' Serena piped up as we all sat on the oval. 'We are meeting at 0300 at the park near Ariella's home. Now here is a blue print of the house,' she said spreading out a sheet before us.

'How'd you get that?' I enquired.

'It took me a few hours but I managed to hack a few websites,' she said with a shrug. 'Now this is the back door which leads into the kitchen. I will stay by the door while the rest of you go in. Once you're out of the kitchen it leads into the hallway. Chantelle this is where you'll stop, the others continue,' she said pointing out the areas. 'We turn this corner here; Jordan you guard there. Now at the end of this hall is the study where the safe is located. I'm assuming the locket is as well. Now

Jay you will guard the door while Eva and Ariella enter. Understood?'

I nodded. She made it sound so simple. Too simple.

'You like the plan?' Serena asked. 'Do you think it will work?'

'No,' I said. Serena looked hurt. I quickly continued. 'Yes, it's an excellent plan and it would work but we aren't doing it. Arya told me that Jareth has had the locket for years but he doesn't know how to use it so there is no rush. There is no need, in fact, to break in to someone's house and steal a necklace.'

'Ariella?' Serena said, looking confused.

'I have to go to class,' I interrupted and before she could argue with me, I got up and walked away. As I went to my class, the dream from the night before played in my mind. *Among friends lie enemies* I whispered to myself. What did she mean?

CHAPTER TWELVE

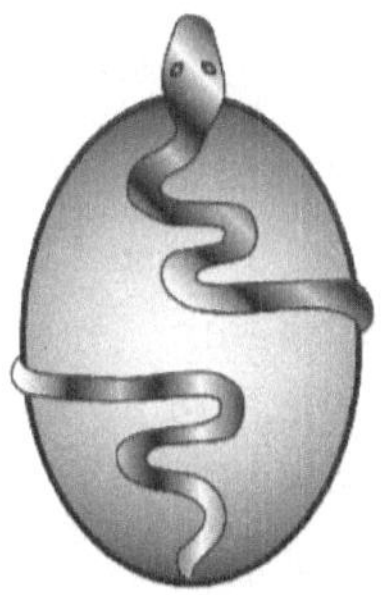

The clock ticked after midnight as I stood at my window looking down into the street below. The light from my lamp revealed my reflection in the glass. I opened the window and allowed the cold night air to blow through my hair. I was beyond nervous. I heard my door open but I didn't turn.

'Can't you sleep?' Aurora asked. I turned to face her; she stood in the doorway holding the door half open.

'I have a lot on my mind,' I replied softly.

She smiled gently at me. 'Just try to sleep,' she whispered before she closed the door.

I sat on my bed and watched the clock tick closer to 3 am. The realisation of what I was about to do dawned on me. I threw some jeans and a singlet on while I continued to mentally prepare myself for this mission.

As the second hand ticked by on the clock, everything in my mind went out of focus. I had three days until I came of age. I thought about the little bit of magic Arya showed me – I wanted to taste it again. I looked over at the clock that now read 2 am. I sat at my desk and pulled out a piece of paper.

Dear Aurora, I wrote and then hesitated.

I closed my eyes and took a deep breath. This was just a precaution in case I didn't come back. I put the pen to paper again.

You always said I had to write my own story, but you've always written it for me. It is now my turn with the pen. I love you, Ariella.

I folded the letter and hoped that I would have returned before she entered my room in the morning. I walked over to the door and put my ear to it – the house was silent. Tiptoeing over to my window, I looked out. I climbed out and slid down to the edge of the roof. Silently, I stood up to climb onto a tree branch and navigated my way down to the ground. The night air was cold against my skin but I didn't really pay much attention. My adrenaline was running wild. I walked past the park I was meant to meet my friends in but I didn't feel guilty about lying to them. I needed to keep them safe and out of danger. I didn't know or trust that I could pull this off myself, but if they got hurt, the guilt would've killed me. I walked to the white house on Everson Road in silence.

'I can do this,' I whispered to myself as I stood across the street from the house. I looked around and made sure no other houses had their lights on or had heads out the window watching me.

I walked further down the street, staying in the cover of the trees. When I was out of view of the house, I crossed the road and walked back towards it. I didn't want to cross the road in front of it in case someone saw me. I snuck around to the rear of the house to the back gate. I stood on my toes to unlatch the lock, but it swung open. Why wasn't it locked? I slipped through the small gap, not wanting to open the gate any further, in case it drew attention. I stopped in my tracks when I saw the back door was open, and slowly turned around to slip back out the gate when I heard someone whisper my name. I jumped and looked back towards the open door where Serena and Eva were standing.

'What are you doing here?' I snapped in a frantic whisper as I walked up to the back door.

'We knew you were lying about not needed to do this,' Eva whispered. 'We know you thought you needed to protect us.'

'Let's go,' Serena said before I could argue. 'The others are already scouting the house.'

We walked through the back door that lead to the kitchen. I walk into the hallway and found it empty; I looked at Serena with concern written all over my face.

'You and Eva go to the office, it's down the hall,' Serena whispered. 'I'll go find the others.'

I went to argue but Serena quickly disappeared around a corner. I looked to Eva who pulled me down the hallway. We walked as silently and quickly as we could.

We finally made it to the study. It had large red doors with gold knobs. The safe would have to be in this one. I reached out for the handle. The gold felt like ice beneath my fingers. As silently as I could I turned the knob and swung the door open. The room was dark and empty, or so it seemed. Eva and I stepped into the room and closed the door behind us. I felt a small amount of comfort knowing Eva was with me. She stood on our side of the door and watched as I walked forward . . . alone.

I reached the desk and ran my fingers over the cold wood. Circling around behind the desk I looked at the large photo that sat on the wall. I froze, shock and disgust flooding through me. He was the guy from the party, the one who put me in hospital. I studied the photo and noticed I never got a good look at him while at the party. He was handsome, a surfer tan but more natural, his hair was black as ebony and what you would find in an 80's rock band. He wore a dark grey button up shirt which was tight and showed the definition of his toned physique. I turned from the photo and went back to the desk. I rummaged through the desk drawers but there was nothing but paper and office supplies. I felt under the desk to see if there were any locks for hidden compartments.

I shrugged to Eva.

'Try the frame,' she mouthed.

'What?' I said more to myself but turned back to the photo to attempt it anyway.

I traced the edge of the frame and pulled it forward. Behind the photo was hidden a small cabinet. The was no lock or safe to be broken, just a pull open cabinet. I scoffed in amazement. Pulling the cabinet door open I found myself seeing what I was searching for.

I picked up a bronze chain with a moonstone pendant. A gold snake coiled around it, a bright glow shone from the stone. I turned it over in my hand and read the engraving.

'Talen'i'palurin.'

I turned back to Eva who was smiling at me.

'How'd you know that it would be behind the painting?' I asked her as I reached her.

'I read it in a book once. The bad guy hides his safe behind a big horrible painting,' she said.

As I dropped the chain around my neck an alarm filled the room. Eva and I ran out into the hall and I looked around hoping to see Serena. We ran the same path we used to come in and out the kitchen door. Relief filled me when I saw the back gate was still open. We ran across the road and into the cover of the trees.

'Where did everyone go?' I asked as we sat down in the shadows.

I suddenly saw Serena running out the gate, so I stepped forward to show her our hiding space. She ran into my arms and we returned to the cover of the trees. In the distance I saw Jordan. I screamed out to him but Serena and Eva pulled me back. Turning to argue with them I saw two men in black and red uniforms walked past. We stayed silent in our hiding spot. I watched the guards through the bushes. They were carrying guns. I looked back to where I saw Jordan but he was now nowhere to be seen.

As we sat behind the trees my heart raced with fear. We watched and waited as the men walked back into the yard. With a burst of anger, I went to jump up and run back to the house but Eva pulled me back down and covered my mouth. Moments later more men in red and black uniforms covered the yard, obviously looking for us. There was no way we were getting back into that house. As the men dispersed back into the house we ran into the back streets that held more trees to cover our movement. A surge of power called out to me. I looked around trying to sense where it was coming from but I saw more men in uniform so we continued to run.

By the time we reached the park and I was gasping for air. I fell to my knees to let the cool breeze wash over me. The pendant still felt cold against my skin; I was not sure how that was possible. I pulled it out from beneath my singlet and looked it over. Serena and Eva sat beside me, watching.

'Who would ever have thought something so beautiful could be so dangerous?' Serena whispered as I hid it beneath my singlet again.

'What do we do now?' I asked.

'We sneak into our houses and talk about this at school. Jay and Chantelle's parents aren't home and Jordan's are on holidays,' Serena said as she stood up and brushed herself off.

'Are you kidding me?' I snapped, trying not to yell. 'We can't just leave them there; we have to call the police or break back in or...'

'We can't call the cops,' Serena cut in. 'We are the ones that broke in, and we can't break back in because there are too many people in the back yard. There is no way we can get back in. We have to go home, lie low, rest and think over a new plan in the morning.'

'Why did you guys come?' I yelled, tears welling up in my eyes. 'I told you the plan was off. You were protected.'

Eva embraced me as I started to cry. I fell to my knees again, Eva's arms still around me. Serena knelt down in front of us. 'We'll get them back.'

I looked up at her. She was blurry from the tears in my eyes. I wiped away my tears as Eva released me from the hug and we all stood up. I took a deep breath to calm myself down; I didn't know where those tears came from.

'Now let's go home,' Serena said to me again. 'We will regroup first thing in the morning. We'll both come to your house before school.'

I nodded and we all walked the streets with limited talking. I insisted on walking Eva home before Serena and I got on our way. I had already got three of my friends in trouble and I didn't want anyone else to.

When I snuck into my room. The first thing I noticed was a letter on my bed. I opened it to see four words: *I told you so.*

CHAPTER THIRTEEN

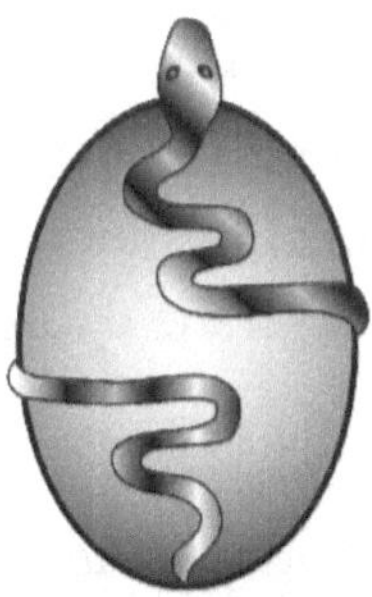

I heard arguing coming from downstairs. I sat on my favourite step and watched Arya and Aurora in the kitchen.

'You could kill him and Ariella could stay safe and out of Alesmera,' Aurora said.

'I can't,' Arya replied darkly.

'What do you mean you can't? I thought you were strong enough?'

'Against Jareth?' Arya scoffed. 'I could kill that spoilt brat in a heartbeat, but I won't.'

'But Ariella will die if she faces him. You must kill him.'

'NO!' Arya banged her fist on the table and leaned over to Aurora. 'If I kill him it will bring around another supernatural war. We are still trying to recover from that. Do you really want to start another one?'

Aurora sagged down into the chair. She looked exhausted as though she hadn't been sleeping. Looking over to Arya who was pacing the kitchen she asked, 'Do you still care for him?'

Arya looked at Aurora with a look saying didn't it matter. Arya kneeled before her and took her hand. 'Ariella is strong. I'll keep her safe,' Arya whispered.

'How do you propose to do that?' Aurora asked.

'With our blood connection,' Arya said. Aurora looked at her as though she'd forgotten that was an option.

What's a blood connection? I wondered.

Aurora stood up and walked out of the kitchen. I quickly ran back up the stairs and into my room. I jumped into bed and pulled the blanket right up under my chin, curling up on my side, I heard the door open. I closed my eyes and pretended to be asleep. The foot of the bed sank under Aurora's weight as she sat down. She sat there for a moment in silence before standing up and walking out.

CHAPTER FOURTEEN

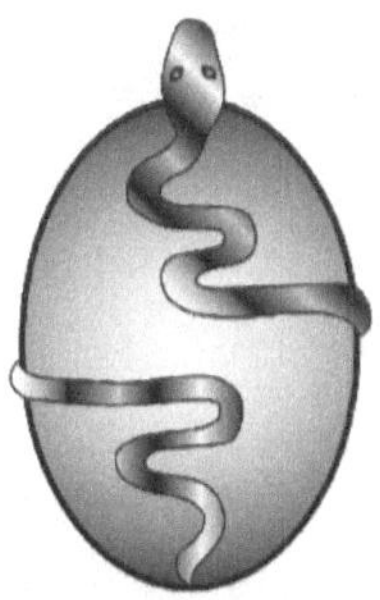

The next morning arrived and I was lying in bed staring at the ceiling. What was I going to do? How was I going to get Jordan, Jay and Chantelle back? There was a soft knock at the door so I sat up. Eva and Serena walked in, all ready for school, and I realised I should probably do the same.

'Ariella, what are we going to do?' Serena asked as she sat down at the foot of my bed. 'I went by their houses this morning, they aren't there.'

I sighed and put my head in my hands.

'What will he do to them?' Eva asked, as she stood by the door.

From downstairs I heard the front door open and close. It would be Aurora going out for the morning. I remembered her conversation with Arya from the night before. Without a word to Eva or Serena I got up and left my room. I walked to the other side of the hall and opened the guest room door without even knocking. Arya was sitting on the window sill, her nose in a book. She didn't even look up at my entrance.

'Take me to Alesmera,' I demanded.

A knowing smile played upon her lips, like it always did. She knew this would happen. She knew I would end up in Alesmera. I stood there waiting for her to answer but she didn't look up. I scoffed and stormed back to my room, slamming the door.

'What was that?' Serena asked.

'He would have taken them to Alesmera, where I was born; where he is from. Only she knows how to get in because there is no way Aurora will show me.'

'Who is she?' Eva asked.

'Arya.'

I turn around and saw her standing in the doorway. I hadn't even heard the door open.

'Are you going to help us?' I asked.

'I will show you the gatekeeper that'll allow you into Alesmera, but I will not enter. You go in alone,' Arya said softly, not breaking eye contact.

'We're coming,' Eva piped up.

Arya shrugged. 'Your choice.'

The front door opened again and I heard Aurora's voice. Arya looked back at the staircase and back at me.

'You three use the window, meet me across the street from the house you lost your friends at, but keep cover in the trees. Don't let anyone see you. I will tell Aurora you've gone to school and also pack my stuff in the process because when you don't come home tonight, I'd rather not get the blame,' Arya said, before leaving to walk downstairs.

We successfully managed to climb out the window, and went around to the front of the house. As we passed the kitchen window I peeked through and saw Yvette and Tatiana with Aurora.

'Who are they?' Serena asked.

'They are the women who told me who I was,' I whispered.

'When this is over, thank them for me' Serena said, I turn and see her smiling.

'I know our plan didn't go . . . to, well, plan but we got the locket,' Eva said. I felt the chains around my neck: the locket of my parents' and the one I'd stolen last night.

I looked into the kitchen again and saw Arya enter. She smiled at the three women.

'Yvette it's a pleasure to see you again. I've been meaning to talk to you. Can we step outside for a moment?' Arya said.

They stepped out the front door, I pressed myself against the house hoping they wouldn't see me. I secretly thanked Aurora for having a gardening addiction because I would have been spotted instantly otherwise.

'I need you to stay with Aurora tonight,' Arya said to Yvette. 'I am taking Ariella to Alesmera, so she can carry out her destiny.'

'And how are you going to assist?' Yvette asked.

'I will show her Styr's door and keep the blood connection open, that's all,' she said then walked back inside.

I took one last look inside the kitchen at Aurora then walked away.

We walked to Jareth's in silence. Hiding in the place I stood the first time I saw this place, all the memories of the previous night rushed at me and the darkness overwhelmed me.

'Are you alright?' I heard Serena ask before I fell unconscious.

The dream had a familiar feel. I found myself in the school hall with Jessica the day I accidentally zapped her. This time I got a proper look at her face. When it happened it looked as though she got freaked out, but now she looked excited. Did she know?

I woke to Arya's hand connecting to my face.

'What the hell are you doing?' I said as I sat up. We were still in front of the mansion, hidden under the trees.

'If you feel the darkness, pull away. Don't fall into it,' Arya exclaimed. She stepped away from me and muttered, 'Idiot girl.'

Serena and Eva helped me up. I brushed myself off and followed after Arya who had walked off. We followed her through the trees that kept us out of sight of anyone looking out the mansions windows. She stopped at the edge of his yard.

'Do you see it?' she asked me.

I looked into the forest. I could see Jareth's men standing within the trees but I know that wouldn't be what she was talking about. I looked around them and that's when I saw it, a blue light in the shape of a doorway.

'See what?' Serena asked.

'It's a doorway, right there,' I said pointing to it.

'They can't see it,' Arya said. 'It's only visible to those with magic.'

She pulled out a pen and piece of paper and wrote something down. She folded the paper and handed it to me.

'When I take care of the guards, go through the door and give this to the keeper,' she said before she turned and started walking towards the guards.

I looked from her to the guards, there were four of them and one of her. She turned and winked at me then continued to walk towards them. She walks up to them, then, before they realised what she was doing, she kicked one of them in the stomach, while throwing a knife she had grabbed from her boot at another. I watched in amazement at how elegant she looked whilst fighting the guards. None of them even got close to wounding her. She had three of them unconscious and one pinned down. We ran over to her.

'Jareth is in Alesmera,' she whispered as the guard fell unconscious.

'What's a blood connection?' I asked her as she got up to walk away. She paused for a moment then continued to walk away. I wanted to say thank you but I knew I didn't have time to run after her.

CHAPTER FIFTEEN

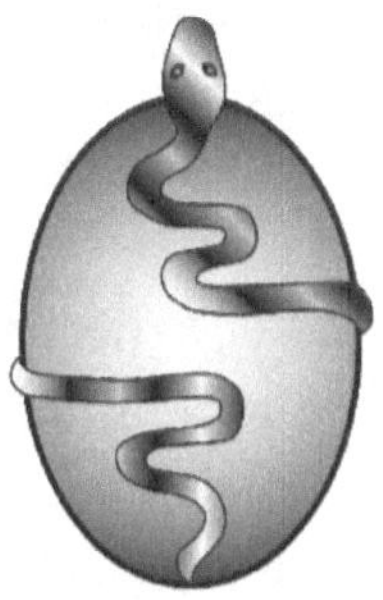

I took hold of Serena and Eva. Hand-in-hand, the three of us walked through the mystical door. I felt a tingle rush over me as we walked through the blue light. When we reached the other side we found ourselves in what looked like a wooden cabin. The only things in the room were a black leather couch, a clock on the wall and a door.

I heard the door open and I turned to see a middle aged man with black shoulder length hair and dark brown, almost black eyes. His arms were covered with tattoos. I could see Indian heads and cross and bones. He wore a tight black singlet with dark grey jeans and a long black coat.

He looked at me with such curiosity in his eyes that he didn't even notice my friends.

'Atlanta, could it be?' he whispered.

'This is from Arya,' I said handing him the letter. I tried to hide my nerves.

'Please step into my room,' he said as he read the letter. I walked into the room with a quick glance back at Serena and Eva who looked as nervous as I felt. As I stepped through the doorway the door closed automatically behind me. He leaned against his desk and wrote something on a piece of paper. He then folded it and threw it in the fire place.

'Fire letter,' he said with his back still to me. 'It's the quickest way for creatures such as us to communicate.'

I glanced at the clock; it was already sunset. That was not possible.

'Travel into the magic realm takes longer than a few seconds. It feels like minutes but actually takes a few hours. There are faster ways but this was the safest,' he said turning back to me.

I glanced around the room; it was almost identical to the other one. I kept an eye on the stranger who was now circling me.

'Who are you?' I whispered.

'Styr, at your service,' he said with a smile that made me nervous. 'How I wished to meet you one day. Your mother had such amazing power. May I read yours?'

'I don't have my powers,' I said automatically but realised I was beginning to taste them.

He laughed. 'Just because you are not active doesn't mean the energy isn't there. I wish to compare you to your mother.'

I met his eyes, this time without fear, 'Do it' I whispered.

He placed his hand over my heart and I felt energy travel throughout my body.

'You're more powerful than your mother,' he said as he sat down on the couch. 'Just remember, words are the strongest power.'

'Words are the strongest power,' I whispered back to myself.

I heard the door open behind me. I turned to see the boy from the party, from the painting in the study. Jareth.

'Miss Atlanta, is it?'

'Yes, it is,' I said sharply. 'We forgot introductions when you were seducing and attempting to kill me.'

I hear Styr stand from the couch.

'My Lord, I. . .' Styr stammered, fear in his voice.

'Silence,' Jareth hissed.

'How'd you enter Alesmera?' he asked me, his cold voice fell over my whole body.

I searched my brain for an answer. Arya said not to mention her but I couldn't think of a lie. He walked up to me and grabbed my chin, making me face him.

'How did you enter?' he asked again, more forcefully.

'Arya,' I whispered.

He released my chin and swore beneath his breath. 'Where is the necklace child?' he demanded.

'I don't have it,' I lied.

He pointed out at the door which now showed a green hedge maze, and beyond that, at the end, was a white castle.

'That is my home; not that mortal coil you robbed,' he said, his arm still outstretched. 'That is where your friends are. If you don't give me the necklace you will never see them again.'

This place felt familiar, a bit like home. A surge of bravery came over me, even though I was sure he would kill me this very moment. I looked at him and smiled. 'I'll see them again, and keep the necklace.'

He laughed and disappeared into thin air.

I turned around but Styr and the room were gone. I looked down into the maze. I was alone, with Serena and Eva now on my rescue list. I had no idea what I was doing but I had to do it. Everyone believed in me. Now I had to believe in myself.

CHAPTER SIXTEEN

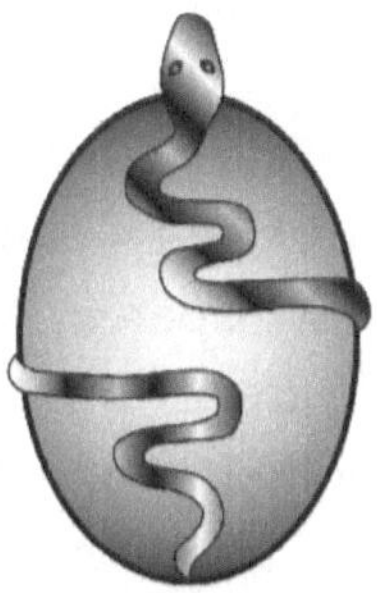

I walked across the bridge leading to the entrance among the hedges. Peering into the maze I found myself staring at a white stone path with never-ending green walls. I stepped into the maze and looked to my left and right, they looked the same. I turned to my left and began to run. I kept running but I didn't see any turns.

I leant back on one of the hedge walls, when suddenly I fell backwards onto the floor. I looked up as the gap I fell through closed back up.

'What are you doing here?' said a voice from behind me which made me jump.

I turned and looked the person before me up and down. He had a dark tunic and cloak on, his eyes were ocean grey and his ears were pointy.

'What are you?' I whispered looking over his pale skin, blonde hair and black eyeliner which gave him a dark, cold look.

'That's a bit rude,' he said, offended. 'You don't ask people what they are – now who are you?' he demanded.

'Ariella,' I replied. 'Ariella Atlanta.'

He took a small step backwards. 'The Ariella? Daughter of Cassandra?'

I nodded.

His grey eyes held such curiosity. He offered his hand which I took. Once I stood he placed a kiss upon my hand and whispered. 'We elves stand by the Atlanta line. We are at your service.'

'An elf?' I questioned. 'Are there more of you?'

'Yes your majesty. Your mother befriended a young she-elf, Nefertiti and we made Alesmera our home. Though I have not heard from Nefertiti or her offspring for some time'

'Your majesty?' I asked confused.

'You are the daughter of the king, the true heir to the throne.'

I laughed nervously. 'I suppose I am. Which way to the castle?'

'Just follow the maze north.'

He released my hand and I turned to start navigating the maze again but noticed the elf fall into step beside me.

'Can I help you?' I asked as kept walking.

'I am assisting you in...whatever you're doing,' he replied plainly.

I smiled. 'I am finding my way to the castle to confront Jareth,' I said with determination.

'You can't do it like that,' he said looking at me.

I looked at him offended.

'I mean you stand out.'

With that comment I looked down at my singlet and jeans and compared it to his outfit. He had a point.

'How do I fix that?' I asked.

'Follow me,' he said with a smile. 'I'm Jace by the way.'

I followed him through the maze, trying to remember every turn we took because I couldn't work out if we were getting closer or further away from the castle. In the middle of all the green we came to a wooden door, which I followed Jace through. He walked over to a chest and pulled out a bag. I looked around and saw that this place didn't look lived in. There was a bed in the far corner and a closet. It looked too tidy.

He brought me the bag and pointed to the room down the hall. 'You can change in that room.'

I felt like it took forever but I finished my disguise. I looked at myself in the mirror; I was wearing a black corset dress with knee high boots – I also had a loose belt which held a small silver dagger, a black strap across my chest which held a sword, a bow and some arrows. I didn't recognise myself at all. I walked out the room and back to where Jace was waiting for me by the door.

'You look amazing your highness.'

'You don't have to call me that,' I said, blushing.

'Until Nefertiti's heir takes the throne, it is you we follow,' he said.

We stepped back outside and I heard a soft whisper in the wind. I turned to Jace but he didn't seem to notice it. I followed the sound with Jace on my heels. After many corners I found it, a hole in the ground at a dead end in the maze. I knelt down before it.

'I can hear something coming from down here,' I said as I put my legs in the hole, preparing to enter.

I took a deep breath and jumped. The air around me felt thick as I fell. I didn't dare open my eyes. It felt like seconds before I hit the ground. I pushed myself off the ground and dusted off my clothes. I looked up and called out to Jace. I saw him take a deep breath before he jumped into the darkness. He made it look much more graceful though.

We stood in an underground tunnel with only one way to walk. I went to take a step but he grabbed my arm.

'Shh, just wait,' he whispered. I glanced back at him but his eyes were focused on the darkness in front of us. I looked back down the tunnel. It took my eyes a moment to adjust to the lack of light but then I saw him, Jareth.

'My darling,' he whispered, as he walked over to us and stood uncomfortably close to me. 'I see you've found these creatures,' he said distastefully looking at Jace. He turned back to me. 'How are you enjoying our lost world?'

'It feels like home,' I whispered.

His finger stroked my lips and he bent down to gently kiss my cheek. 'Why don't I make it more fun?'

He threw a green spark behind us and we heard a crash. We turned around and saw the walls caving in. Jareth had disappeared and we had no choice but to run. Jace was ahead of me, scouting our exit, but before I could catch up, the ground beneath me collapsed and I fell into the shadows.

CHAPTER SEVENTEEN

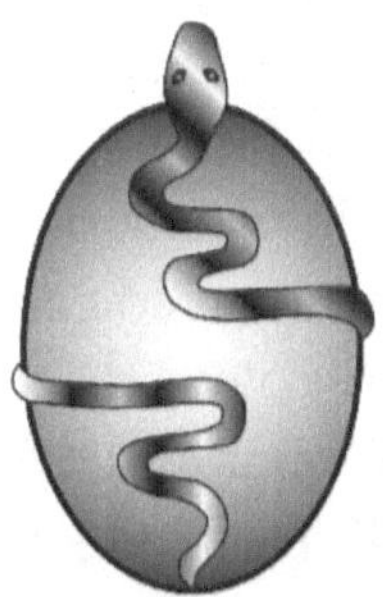

I woke up on a dirt floor in a small room, aching. I pushed myself off the ground and dusted the dirt from myself. A sharp pain shot up my arm when I moved it. I put my hand to it and felt wetness. Was I bleeding?

I looked up at the darkness that I just fell through. I wanted to call out to Jace but I didn't know what else could be in this room with me.

'Words are the strongest power,' I whispered, remembering what Styr had said to me. I repeated the quote to myself again and again until words started to form on my tongue.

'Give me light,' I murmured. Red sparks ignited from my hands and the candles in the room lit up with small, golden flames.

The room was small and circular containing only a single wooden door with a golden knob. I walked over to the door and pushed it open revealing a spiral staircase. I glanced back into the empty room and closed the door behind me. The candles within the staircase flickered which gave me hope that there was an exit nearby. Candles flickered when there was wind, right? I kept circling down the staircase. I caught my breath out of amazement when I came to the bottom. I had expected another door to another room. I hadn't expected a golden, engraved gazebo followed by a rainforest of vibrant colour.

I gazed into the rainforest I fell into and felt at home. I walked through the trees, their trunks showered in flower petals. I heard running water. Following the sound, I noticed how dry my mouth was. I found a waterfall and stopped in my tracks; it was the same one from my dreams. I looked around to make sure no one was around before stepping out into the open. I walked over to the water and knelt on the grass before it. I cupped water into my hand and drank. It was the most amazing water I had ever tasted, though I thought that was just because I was very thirsty. I jumped onto rocks to reach the other side of the river. I gazed around at the beauty that surrounded me and just took a moment to breathe.

I heard laughter from up ahead. Cautiously I rested my hand on the knife on my belt and walked forward. I found an emerald green meadow; I hid in the shadows of the trees and looked at the cherry blossom tree that sat in the centre of the field. Surrounding the tree were seat-like stumps. Upon one sat a black cat and the other a young man. He wore a black and blue checked shirt with a vest and dark jeans. Upon his head sat a stylish hat; something about him made my heart begin to race.

It seemed foolish to stay hidden. It wasn't getting me anywhere so I stepped out from the shadows. I walked towards the tree. The young man stood up and I might have been imagining it but I thought I saw amazement in his eyes.

'Cassandra,' he exhaled as I reached him.

'You knew my mother?' I asked.

'You're not Cassandra?' he asked, with a confused look on his face.

'Her daughter,' I replied, feeling jealous that everyone here but me knew my mother. 'Ariella.'

He raised his hand to brush a strand of hair behind my ear. 'This isn't a life I wanted you to find.'

He took my hand and led me over to a stump chair on which I sat cross legged. There were miniature humans with wings among the cherry blossoms chattering in a foreign tongue I didn't understand. They looked devious with their blonde hair, pale skin and green eyes.

'They say you're very pretty,' said the young man as he sat down beside me. He took his hat off and brushed his brunette hair back, though it just fell back down around his face. 'I'm Zed Hale. Most people call me by my last name.'

I smiled as I repeated his name in my mind. Zed Hale.

'What are they?' I asked, pointing to the miniature humans.

'Tree Fairies' he said with a soft laugh. 'Not the granting wishes kind that are in children books but small immortal beings who are more powerful than they look.'

'There's different types of fairies?' I asked.

He nodded. 'Yes, of course. In some lands there are even fairies that are mistaken for humans.'

'The crimson,' said a deep voice. I looked around and saw no one else. Then I looked to the black cat, confused. I knew animals didn't talk, but who else could have said it?

'You're bleeding,' Hale said. He knelt before me and examined my arm. Wiping away the blood, I realised how bad it was. He wrapped it up in a black bandage and placed a kiss upon it which sent shivers through my body.

'Thank you,' I whispered as I looked into his golden eyes, unable to break eye contact. I felt my heart racing and my breathing getting heavier.

'Incoming,' the deep voice said. I looked back at the cat who was looking into the trees. I followed the direction of his gaze and saw a small fox-like creature running towards us.

'What news?' said the voice, it was definitely the cat.

'Guards came through the gazebo, they seek the girl,' the fox said between breaths.

'Thank you Laszlo,' Hale said to the fox.

He pressed a small button on the side of my tree stump and before I realised what had happened I found myself inside my tree stump chair. From below I listened to the silence, then heard hooves. Horses approached.

'Have you seen the girl?' said a female voice I recognised but couldn't place.

'What girl?' I heard the cat ask in his deep voice.

'The one Jareth has solving his maze you fool,' snapped the female.

'She was not meant to enter this part of the realm, she was meant to stay in the maze,' said a cold male voice. 'Have you perhaps seen an elf with a female companion?'

'An elf?' Hale questioned.

'We have not seen a girl or any elves,' Hale said clearly and firmly.

I listened as the horses rode away. The top of the stump opened and Hale helped me out.

'Sorry for dropping you without warning, but we can't have you found,' Hale explains.

'Its fine,' I said, as I stood up. I lost my balance and fell into Hale, who caught me. My skin felt warm where we touched. My heart was beating so loud that I feared he could hear it. I'd never felt like this before, and not to sound like a silly girl with a crush but it felt amazing.

'It's an honour to meet you,' said Laszlo, and I unwillingly stepped out of Hale's arms.

'Let me introduce myself,' said the cat, his green eyes looked me over. 'My name is Samir, and I was a trusted companion of your mother.'

'Can you tell me about her?' I asked as I sat on the grass.

'She was. . .' he paused, as though looking for a word grand enough to describe her, 'like sunshine. She simply had to walk in the room and everything would be better. We felines mourned her death for many moons.'

'But what was she like?' I asked, trying not to sound emotional. 'I don't know anything about her. Aurora would never tell me.'

Samir looked to Hale then back to me; his eyes held mine. 'She was the bravest and kindest person you would ever meet. She always put everyone else first, helping them in any way she could. She always saw the best in people.'

I glanced up at Hale and caught him gazing at me with a look I could almost guess as adoring. I smiled and wondered what he was thinking. I turned away from those perfect, kissable lips that were smiling at me.

'Let's walk,' Hale said, offering his hand which I took without hesitation.

'I'll see you two tonight,' he said before we walked away from the cat and the fox. I hoped I was making the right decision to go with him.

CHAPTER EIGHTEEN

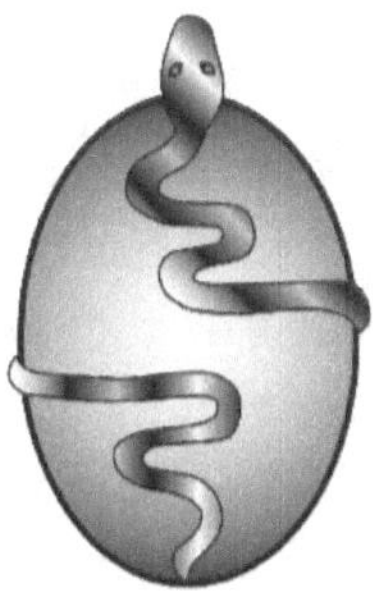

Hale and I walked in silence at first. I was unsure of what to say. I had too many questions but was too nervous to ask.

'Your mother was an amazing woman,' Hale said to me when we were in the trees, away from the meadow.

'What were you to her?' I asked.

'Cassandra and my mother were best friends,' he said. I could tell he was remembering her as he spoke. 'You perhaps know her. Her name is Tatiana.'

I nodded.

'What's tonight?' I asked.

'It's nothing important; my mother is hosting a party,' he said. 'Would you like to come?'

'I can't, I need to find my friends,' I said with regret.

He stopped and stood before me. 'Come with me tonight and I promise, first thing tomorrow I will help you find your friends'

I looked at him as though he was crazy. Did he really think I'd give up looking for my friends to go to a party? They could have been tortured for all I knew.

'We both know you have no idea how to get to the castle. If we made an appearance at my mother's party for a few hours and then went to the castle, I guarantee you that we would get there faster than if you went off by yourself now.'

I smiled, 'I'd love to experience an Alesmera party.'

We walked through the forest for what felt like hours. I was beginning to feel faint and my mouth was parched. As we came to a clearing I gasped at the sight of a white stone mansion with a multitude of windows.

'Wow,' escaped my lips. 'You grew up here?'

'It's not as fabulous as it looks,' he mumbled under his breath.

Hale rang the doorbell and we waited. I saw Tatiana's look of shock when she answered the door.

'Ariella, I'm so glad you're here,' she said, quickly recovering herself. 'Let's take you upstairs and find you a dress.'

I followed her up the stairs whilst Hale stayed on the ground floor. We walked into what I assumed to be a bedroom but was actually a giant wardrobe.

'Take your pick,' Tatiana said.

The colours were amazing. I didn't know that this many colours existed. I walked around the room admiring each dress. I stopped at a sapphire blue dress with a diamante V neckline. I pulled it out and stood in front of the full length mirror.

'That is perfect,' Tatiana said with what sounded like fake excitement. 'Especially with your eyes.'

'Tatiana,' I heard someone call. 'Have you not chosen a dress yet?'

The voice stopped in the doorway. Yvette looked at me with amazement and joy. She waltzed over and embraced me.

'Go prepare your party Tatiana,' Yvette said turning back to her. 'I will help the guest of honour get ready.'

Tatiana smiled nervously at Yvette before leaving. Yvette turned back to me with a smile.

'I'm so glad that you made it here safely,' Yvette said in a hushed whisper as she made sure the dress fit perfectly. Her fingers played with my hair and I wondered if I would look like I did when Serena used me as her doll.

'Why are you whispering?' I asked.

She met my eyes for a moment. 'There are spies everywhere. Tatiana is under a lot of pressure because many of her guests are Jareth's followers. I mustn't be seen by most because they know I follow your mother but I always come help Tatiana set up.'

'Why isn't Tatiana a known follower of my mother's?' I asked.

Yvette looked sad. 'Because of her kids. The rebels are treated brutally if caught, so she lied and saved her children's future.'

I looked at her as if to ask *why do you risk coming here*? Tatiana had loyalties to her children, yes, but she still chose to turn her back on my mother.

'It was always the three of us,' she said sadly. 'I lost your mother. I couldn't lose two best friends.'

When Yvette was sure that she was finished I stole a glance in the mirror to find long silver earrings hiding within my pulled back curls, only two strands of hair hung before my face. The dress showed the outline of my hour glass figure. I didn't recognise myself, I looked . . . royal.

A knock at the door pulled me from my reflection and I smiled when I saw Hale standing in the doorframe. Yvette excused herself and left with only a small nod to Hale.

Hale walked up to me and I found myself holding my breath.

'You look beautiful' he said.

Butterflies filled my stomach!

'Shall we?' he said, offering his hand. I took it and bit my lip to hide my smile. We walked out of the room and down the stairs to the party. I stole a glance in Hale's direction and found myself blushing at his smile.

We reached the bottom of the steps and I turned to him.

'Hale!' screeched a female voice, moments before a gorgeous redhead jumped into his arms and kissed him.

I felt a sharp pang of sadness in my chest as they disappeared into the party. I looked around but Yvette's warning about Jareth's supporters echoed within my mind. I returned to the stairs and just sat, watching the party.

'What a cute couple they make' said a voice. Breaking my gaze from Hale who was across the room with the red head I saw a young brunette in a golden gown sitting beside me. Her green eyes were screaming boredom and distaste.

'Who is a cute couple?' I asked.

'My brother and soon to be sister-in-law,' she sulks. 'You know my brother Hale right? I saw him walk you down the stairs.'

'You're Tatiana's daughter?' I asked.

'Yeah, how do you . . .' she stopped midsentence. 'Wait, are you the girl she crossed over to find?' she said so softly I barely heard her.

'Guilty,' I murmur under my breath.

'Oh my god,' she exclaimed. 'That is so exciting.'

'Did you say sister-in-law?' I interrupted.

Her facial expression turned to annoyance. 'Yes. I don't know why he is marrying her. She is horrible, plus she said she is a witch but she can't even float a pencil.'

Marriage?

I felt my heart drop. I excused myself from the girl and ran upstairs to the dressing room where I left my stuff. I closed the door and was about to take off the dress when I heard loud voices from downstairs.

'Attention,' yelled a female voice. 'Continue with your party, we are just searching for a girl from the mortal world.'

Panic flooded me. I quickly grabbed the bag with my clothes, strapped on my weapons, switched off the lights and hid amongst the dresses. I took a deep breath as I heard the door open. The light flickered on and I stood as still as a statue.

'She isn't here,' said the female voice.

I sighed in relief when the lights turned off and the door closed. But it was short lived. A figure stormed into the room followed by another, who turned the lights back on.

'Jesminda, please stop causing a scene,' Hale said, irritation laced his voice.

'Me,' she shrieked angrily. 'You're the one who has been staring at that filthy mundane creature instead of paying attention to me. What would people think? I am your fiancée, not her.'

Hale put his hand to his forehead and sighed.

'I should turn that little witch in,' Jesminda continued. 'She is going to ruin everything.'

'Everything is ruined whilst Jareth is in charge.'

'Tell me you love me,' she whispered.

He looked up to meet her gaze.

'Tell me,' she begged, taking a step towards him so there was no space between them.

He grabbed her and kissed her. 'I love you,' he whispered as he released her.

'You can't turn her in,' he said as he took a step back away from her.

She scoffed and stormed out of the room. I gazed at him from between the dresses. His hand again rested on his head. I leant against the wall in the wardrobe and supressed the urge to cry at what I had just witnessed. The looks, the feelings, I had imagined them all. He didn't want me. What was wrong with me? First Jareth and now Hale.

Hale finally left the room, closing the door behind him which gave me the chance to escape. I slipped of the heels knowing I'd never be able to run in them. As I stepped out from amongst the dresses, Tatiana's daughter walked in. She closed the door behind her.

'What are you doing?' she asked suspiciously.

'I was planning on running away,' I said honestly.

She smiled at me. She opened the door and peered into the hallway. Looking back at me and she signalled me to follow. I followed her into what

I assumed was her room. She led me over to her wardrobe and pushed aside her clothes which revealed a trap door.

'It's a hidden stair case,' she said proudly. 'When you get out just keep running until you can no longer see white. I've read stories about your Mum and I am prepared to follow you if you are half the person she was.'

'Thank you' I whispered. I opened the trap door and began to navigate my way down the steps. 'Wait, what's your name?'

'Adriana' she whispered. 'I'll keep them distracted as long as I can. Now go.' She closed the trap door and I continued down the stairs and out the door into blinding sunlight. I threw the bag strap over my shoulder and began to run.

CHAPTER NINETEEN

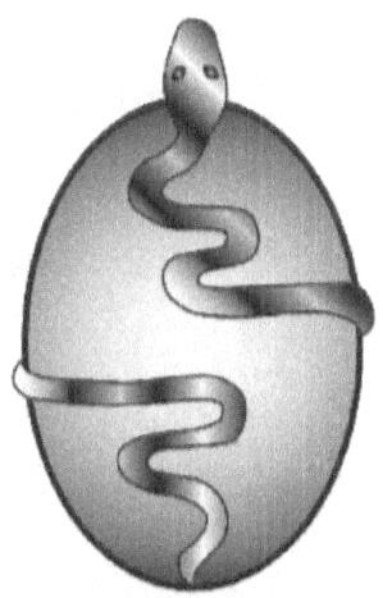

I had to stop running when a stitch caught my side. I heard Hale yelling my name in the distance, but I felt as though I was imagining that. I leant against a tree to rest for a moment. But instead of my back hitting the tree I fell through it.

I landed flat on my back on a dusty wooden floor. I suppressed a groan of pain as I scrambled up and balanced myself. While I brushed myself off I realised I was still in Tatiana's dress. Oops, I wondered if they had dry cleaners here. I heard music coming from upstairs. The room I stood in was lit up with black candles on black walls. The staircase looked old and unstable. I stood on the first step testing to see if it would creak under my weight but everything remained silent. I walked up the steps until I could see into the upstairs room. I thought it was a ballroom full of guests. They looked like people but most of them were blue and transparent.

From the ceiling hung a silver box frame from which a girl in a black corset was doing acrobatics. I walked up a few more steps to get a better view. On the stage below the girl in the silver box were two more girls. Sisters I think, one was red with pigtails and the other had a pink ponytail. The girl in the box had olive skin with long dark curls. The two girls on the stage sang what sounded like a lullaby and I felt myself wanting to go to them.

A dangerous looking man walked from behind the curtains to the edge of the stage and watched the girls for a moment before drawing his hungry gaze over the audience. His red shirt made his hair and eyes seem darker than black. His eyes found mine and a devious smile drew up his lips. I took a step down but stopped when I saw a man with blonde hair down to his shoulders in a black suit walk onto the stage, clapping. He bowed and waved his top hat.

'Attention audience, that is all for this afternoon. Your beautiful sirens here will return tonight at the darkest hour.' He clapped again before leaving the stage.

Without looking back at the man in the red suit I quickly snuck back down the stairs and began searching for an exit.

'Are you lost my sweet?' asked a cold voice.

I turned and saw the man in the red suit before me. I shook my head.

'Just looking for the exit,' I said, my voice steady.

'I can show you,' he said as he stepped closer.

I attempted to run but he pinned me against the wall and pressed his hand over my mouth. I screamed into his hand when he sunk his teeth into my neck.

'Dom,' someone yelled, making him remove his teeth. I whimpered in pain.

'Release her,' the voice continued. 'I claimed her'

Dom released me and I collapsed to the floor. I put my hand to my neck and saw ocean grey eyes before I fell unconscious.

I woke up between dark red sheets in a windowless room.

'Don't get up,' someone said from the shadows. 'You've lost a lot of blood.'

The blonde from the stage came and sat on the bed beside me, lighting a few candles for me to see him clearly. I noticed that he had the same sharp teeth that Dom had. Then I noticed the grey eyes. They were the eyes I had seen before I fell unconscious. A thank you played upon my lips, but I didn't say it.

'What . . . who are you?' I asked, stopping myself from asking what he was.

'Julius Fleetwood,' he said, 'and my question for you Miss Atlanta is how long have you been here?'

He leaned in closer making my heart race. 'How do you know my name?' I murmured.

He smiled making my cheeks flush.

'A few days,' I said, remembering his question.

'And you haven't asked me what I am yet or where you are? You're not a very curious kitten are you?'

'I was told that it is rude to ask someone what they are.'

He laughed, 'I'm a nosferatu.'

I stared at him blankly.

'Vampire,' he said more bluntly. 'You know, children of the night, immortals, dietary requirement of blood – did Aurora teach you nothing before sending you back?'

'Aurora wouldn't tell me anything. Arya brought me here.'

'Arya,' he said with a soft laugh. 'I haven't seen her in years.'

I looked away, irritated, though I wasn't sure why this annoyed me.

'No, we never,' he said. The emotions must have shown on my face. 'She was with Lilith, our red headed siren.'

'What's a siren?' I asked. And geez, Arya got with everyone.

'The three girls on the stage. Their voices are magical. They draw the weak souls into our den and keep them prisoner.'

I wanted to question the morals in that but he leant in and kissed me. He lay his body over mine and entangled his fingers with mine. I melted into his kiss and felt . . . wait, I had to get to the castle. I pushed him off.

'Why do you push me away love?' he asked, his body still hovering over me.

'Because I am not interested in you. I just met you,' I snapped.

He scoffed, 'Don't lie to me kitten. I can hear your heart beat and your blood racing.'

I craved to kiss him again but pushed it out of my mind. 'I have things to do,' I said, more to myself than to him. 'Important things. Life and death important.'

Even as I argued with myself a dark need and hunger arose in me, but before I could think on it more he stood up and the need disappeared. He led me out of the room and I followed him down the corridor. I got the feeling I was walking deeper into the building than out. I questioned where he was leading me but he just told me to follow him. I had no choice in the matter so I followed, a smile playing on my lips as I thought about the kiss we shared.

'Where is this?' I ask as he led me through a door into another bedroom.

I looked around the room. In the corner was a bed and basic bedroom furniture but on the wall in front of me was a large map. He led me over to the table that sat below the map on the wall. I found myself staring at a large scale model of a maze and forest.

'What is this?' I asked, looking at the model.

'It's Alesmera,' Julius said. 'It's Arya's – I figure if you two are associates she wouldn't mind me showing you her room.'

I looked at him with confusion as though asking why Arya had a room here. Julius looked at me for a moment as though he was about to tell me then looked away.

'It's for us to have our own privacy when she is here,' said a soft voice from behind me. I turned to the door and saw Lilith, the red headed girl from the stage, standing there watching us. 'It's also somewhere for her to hide out when she is here. Jareth doesn't allow her into Alesmera.'

'How often is she here?' I asked, wondering why she hadn't entered with me.

'When she needs me,' Lilith said. 'Or when I need her. We met thirty-five years ago. She was hurting, and she heard my voice. My voice drags in the souls of the damned, but she didn't hear that, she heard the pain in my voice.'

She looked down with a small smile on her lips, her thumb traced her lower lip and I knew she was remembering a moment of passion. 'She showed up one day, drenched from the rain. She pointed at me and said 'I want her' then just walked up to me and kissed me.'

Lilith looked up to meet my eyes. Her eyes glistened with tears. 'We saved each other, Arya was very complicated and you'll never work her out.' Without another word, Lilith turned around and left the room.

I looked to Julius, who was looking at the door where Lilith had just exited, wondering whether he should go and see if she was okay. He looked back at me smiling, and indicated to the map. He showed me where we were, and the quickest and safest path to the castle. I took a few minutes attempting to memorise the path.

'I'll show you out,' he said after I turned away from the map.

He offered his hand and I reached out and accepted it, feeling a spark rush into me from the smallest touch. He walked me out of the room, handing me my things and showed me to the inside of a waterfall.

'Are you kidding me?' I exclaimed.

He shook his head. 'The only way out of here is to jump.'

I wanted to scream in frustration. 'Turn around,' I demanded.

He turned around and I slipped out of the blue dress and pulled the dress Jace had given me back on. He turned back around as I was strapping my weapon belt back on. I threw the blue dress and the smaller daggers into the bag but held onto the arrows and bow.

'Are you sure this isn't suicide?' I asked.

He laughed at me. 'Kitten, you are far too beautiful to throw to the bottom of a lake. When you're done with your important things you should come visit me.'

'Don't hold your breath,' I said before jumping.

'I won't but you better,' I heard him yell as I fell into the water. The current pulled me under and through the caves.

CHAPTER TWENTY

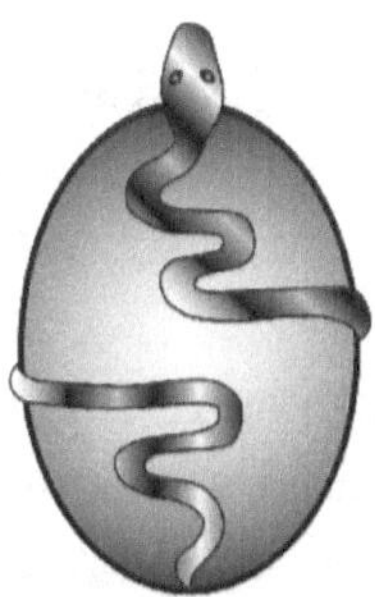

I emerged from the lake gasping for air and
blinked in the brightness of the sun. I struggled to
get to the shore without dropping any of my
weapons.

'Ariella,' I heard a familiar voice call out as I
reached the grass.

I looked up to see Hale running towards me. He
helped me out of the lake and to my feet.

'I've been looking for you for hours. Why are
you. . .' he paused as his eyes saw my neck, 'You
were in the Casa De Los Muertos?'

'The Casa De-la what?' I asked confused.

'You let a nosferatu feed from you,' he exclaimed in disgust.

'I did not,' I argued.

'You've got a scar from their bite on your neck,' he yelled.

'Because Dom attacked me!' I fumed then stormed off.

I heard him jog up behind me. 'Ariella, I apologise. I overreacted. I panicked when I couldn't find you. Why did you leave?'

'Because your fiancé would have turned me in if I stayed.'

'She's not my. . .' I glared at him before he could finish the sentence. 'It's complicated. Witches marry within the circle so we've been engaged since birth.'

'I don't care that you're engaged,' I yelled. Too many emotions welled up inside of me. 'You were flirting with me. You should have told me.'

We heard voices from up ahead which made us both freeze.

'If Jareth learns we lost the girl we will be dead,' said a male voice.

'Don't be foolish,' said the female voice I heard at the house. 'You'll be dead, I won't.'

Hale suddenly grabbed me and pulled me inside a tree. I wondered how many other hollow trees were in this forest and how you could tell them apart. I sat on the high chair that resided in the tree, allowing my feet a moment's rest. Hale stood so close to me that I swore I could feel his heartbeat, which meant he could probably hear mine racing.

I looked up at him and his eyes met mine. I didn't know what compelled me to do it but I leaned forward and kissed him. At first I thought he'd push me away and I would be utterly embarrassed but instead he put his hands in my hair and kissed me more passionately than I could ever have imagined.

He pulled away from me. 'We should find somewhere to rest for the night,' he whispered breathlessly.

Hale opened the door in the tree and I followed him into the night. We came to a tree with a ladder and he signalled for me to climb up.

'Is this where you live?' I asked as we both reached the top. It was a small wooden tree house.

He looked sad. 'I don't want to live with my mother and be surrounded by Jareth's supporters, plus this is how most of your mother's supporters live.'

I looked down at the floor. There was so much conflict residing in this world. Because of my mother's mysterious death, my step brother's need to conquer the world and some unknown queen I apparently knew that wouldn't take her throne. I needed to fix it, even if I didn't know what I was doing.

Hale showed me the bedroom. 'We should get some sleep. You take the bed, and I'll take the floor.'

'I'm sorry,' I blurted out, 'that I kissed you. I don't know what came over me. You're engaged and it can never happen again.'

He gave me a sad smile. 'Let's just get some sleep,' he whispered before getting a blanket and pillow to set himself up on the floor. I fell onto the bed and turned to face him but didn't know what to say. So I just closed my eyes and willed myself to sleep.

As I waited for sleep to claim me, I wondered what it would have been like if my parents had stayed together. If I had grown up with Hale, would we have hated each other as children, been best friends or childhood sweethearts? Would he be engaged to me right now?

I fell into a dream. I was walking through a forest, a place I had never been before, in waking or dreaming. I heard a scream from up ahead so I ran to the edge of the forest and found myself overlooking a war.

I watched a pale girl with piercing red eyes stab a young man. The pale girl walked off, then I saw Arya running out of the lake and towards the young man who just collapsed.

'No, baby, stay with me please. I love you,' Arya cried as she held him in her arms.

The scene changed to a bedroom. A pale man with fangs who reminded me of Dom held a young attractive man. Arya ran into the room and the pale girl took hold of her. As the pale man snapped the attractive man's neck, Arya screamed and the room dissolved around me.

I now stood in a white room with Jareth. 'Did you like intruding on Arya's dream?' he asked me coldly.

'I didn't mean to,' I whispered as he walked over to me.

'You should join me,' he said, taking hold of my arms.

'Never,' I scoffed.

He kissed me and I woke with a sudden jerk.

'What's wrong?' Hale asks.

'Isn't Jareth Aubrey's son?'

Hale nodded, looking confused. Eww, I shivered from disgust, what a bizarre dream.

'I think I was in Arya's dream,' I said, remembering the things I had seen. I didn't realise the pain she had been through. It explained why she was so cold.

'What do you mean in her dream?' Hale asked.

'It was like I was seeing her memories from the sidelines.'

'How is that possible?'

I remembered how she knew when my hand got cut in my dream, and she asked me if I was the one in the white dress or the black dress. She had been in my dreams before. Was this a sign of our blood connection?

CHAPTER TWENTY-ONE

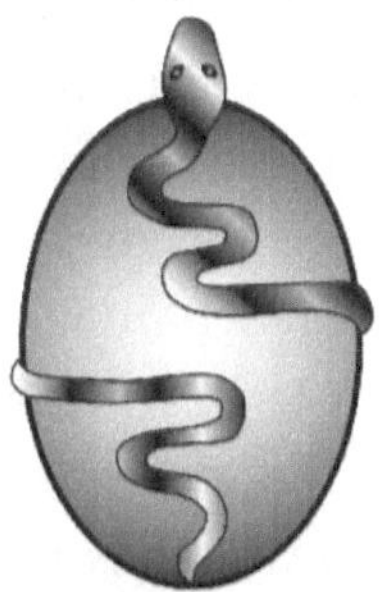

I woke to an empty room and a note on the pillow next to me. I read it silently to myself.

Ariella,

I was summoned home for a coven meeting, I'll be home before midday.

Hale

A covens meeting? More like going home to her. I put aside my jealousy and decided to explore the forest. I put on my weapons belt and threw the bow and arrows on my back. I climbed down the ladder and wandered into the forest.

In the distance something red hidden among all the green, caught my eye. I walked through the tress until I reached an apple tree. It looked like Christmas to me. I ran to the tree without thinking and picked a bright red apple from one of the lower branches. My stomach growled from hunger as I held the apple within my fingers. I took a bite and it was perfectly sweet. I took a second bite, quenching my hunger when suddenly my vision began to blur. I tried to call out for help but I couldn't seem to find my voice. I reached out to the tree for support but all went black.

I stood in a room with mirrored walls and a marble floor. I kept getting pushed around from the sea of dancers around me. I could hear music but couldn't pinpoint where it was coming from. The necklace began to burn from underneath my dress. I pulled out the locket that had the photos but it was ice cold. It was the other locket. I looked around the room but I was not game enough to pull it out so I allowed it to keep burning me. I saw Hale in the distance and pushed my way through the crowd. When I reached him I saw it was just a reflection in the mirror; he wasn't actually there.

'You can have everything you want,' said a voice from behind me, 'if you don't defy me.'

I turned to face Jareth and anger seared though my veins. His hand grabbed my arm and he pulled me to him. He made me dance with him. I saw the faces of the dancers around me and they were all painted skull faces. The necklace continued to burn me beneath my dress.

The dancers' dresses faded to black and turned to body armour. A few of them removed their masks and I saw faces I recognised, Serena and Eva. I watched in horror as the ones who remained masked killed my friends. I tried to pull away from Jareth, who spun me around. Images flashed through my mind. I remembered back to Yvette and Tatiana approaching me in the park; how I felt when the necklace first fell into my hands; the power. How my voice went hoarse from screaming for my friends from the cover of the trees. How Jareth stabbed me in the park. I remembered kissing Hale in the tree.

I remembered the apple.

Jareth was still looking down at me as I lifted my eyes to meet his. I pushed him away and ran to the mirror.

'Let me out,' I screamed as I slammed my fist into the mirror. 'Get out of my head!'

I looked at my broken reflection in the mirror and saw the masked people as they faded into oblivion behind me. The music dwindled into silence. I closed my eyes waiting to wake beneath the apple tree.

I opened my eyes and found myself on a wooden bench surrounded by tree roots that were flickering like a dying lightbulb. I screamed for help but only the sounds of crackling answered me. I was completely alone in a place that felt cursed. I looked around and saw bridges up above in the trees. They didn't look very stable but it sure beat standing on this bench. Now I just had to work out how to avoid the tree roots. I'm not sure if the flickers were an electrical current but I sure didn't want to find out.

With a deep sigh I took a step onto the soft dirt between two roots. Nothing happened. I jumped over the tree roots avoiding the sparks, then out of nowhere a vine whipped out of the ground and grabbed my ankle mid jump, pulling me to the ground. I screamed as I hit a flashing root which left a burn mark on my leg. I pulled myself back into a dirt area but the vine didn't release my ankle.

'Hold on,' called out a voice.

I looked up and a girl with a blonde ponytail swung down and cut the vine from my ankle. She pulled me up, pointed to a ladder on a tree and indicated for me to run to it. She slashed at the vines as they appeared while we ran to the tree with the ladder. When I was midway up the ladder I turned back and saw her beginning to climb, so I went as fast as my body would allow me. I stood on a square metal platform waiting for the blonde girl to reach the top. I looked across the trees and saw a bridge network stretching before me and at the end of each bridge section was another metal platform.

'Thank you,' I said as she reached the top of the ladder and stood up beside me.

As I looked her over I saw that she was an elf. She wore similar attire to Jace and had pointy ears.

'Do you know Jace?' I asked.

She looked at me. 'Yes, I do. He is why I am here. He can't enter this place but I can. I know how to come and go.'

'How did he know I was here?' I questioned.

'He didn't,' she said to me like I was an idiot. 'Her Majesty did. She sensed you falling into this trap and sent a message to Jace who sent it to me.'

I wanted to ask her who Her Majesty was but she signalled me to follow her. She jumped across the bridge without touching a single plank. I looked at her in confusion once she reached the other side.

'When you cross touch as few planks as possible,' she said, but turned around again before I could ask why. I was lucky I excelled in long jump in school and only hit two planks. When I reached the metal square the memory of kissing Hale in the tree and meeting him in the meadow flashed through my mind.

'Are these planks enchanted somehow?' I ask the she-elf.

'Don't think about anything. If you can't control your memories, think of an unpleasant one,' she replied.

'What are you . . .?' I started to ask but she cut me off.

'Talk later, jump now.'

The next bridge was kind of in a downward direction so I hoped I'd only hit one plank. I watched as the elf made another perfect jump. I prepared myself for the jump and amazed myself when I only hit one plank. Again when I fell onto the metal square I remembered a memory. I remembered walking to Tatiana's house with Hale and arguing with him at the lake.

'Hello Miss Atlanta,' I looked up and the she-elf had stopped in her tracks. Jareth stood before us. 'Nancy, can I ask you why you are assisting my prisoner?'

'My Lord, it was her Highness' wishes. I was unaware she was your prisoner. Her Highness did not explain anything to me. She just asked.' Nancy looked down at her feet the whole time she spoke to him.

'You're forgiven,' he snarled. 'Well ladies, I would love to chat but I think I need to seek out a conversation with her Highness. Oh and Ariella, every plank you touch is a memory you lose.' He then vanished and I turned my gaze to Nancy.

'Is he serious?' I yelled.

'I'm sorry I didn't tell you but when you know your mind focuses on your favourite memories and you involuntarily lose them,' Nancy explained. 'There's only one more bridge until the exit.'

I looked past her to the next metal square and saw she was right, there was a door. Without looking at me she turned around and made the last jump. But I hesitated. I was thought back through my life. What memory was I willing to lose? I thought back to my childhood, the memory of when I first asked about my parents. I jumped. When I hit a wooden plank I fell and hit multiple planks, and multiple memories flashed through my mind. I pushed myself up and jumped to the metal square, wondering what memories I'd lost.

'May I ask a favour?' Nancy asked.

'Anything,' I said. She had come here to this awful place to help me when she didn't even know me, I owed her.

'It's just my kid sister was kidnapped and imprisoned in the unclaimed lands. Could you help me save her once your mission is complete?'

'I don't know how much help I'll be, but I will come with you,' I said, knowing I couldn't break my word.

'From here I leave you,' Nancy said. 'I was instructed only to help you out of this place.' She opened the door and stepped through.

'Wait,' I called out and ran after her, but I woke beneath the apple tree. The burn on my leg was now searing. I limped my way back to the lake and entered the water, letting it wash over the burn. I wanted to cry out in pain but bit my lip to suppress the tears. I pulled myself back onto the bank and lay on the grass to rest for just a moment but I fell asleep.

CHAPTER TWENTY-TWO

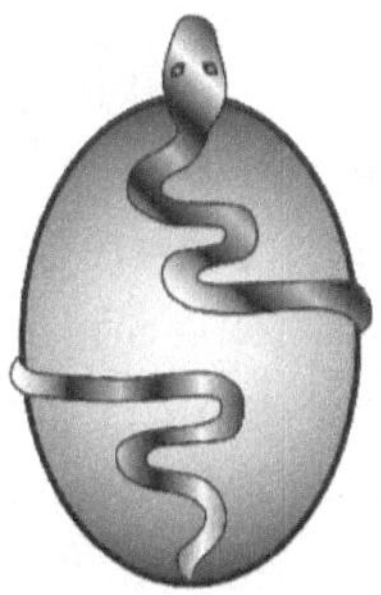

The first thing I felt upon waking was the burning of my skin. It looked to be midmorning which meant I slept through the hottest part of the day. I felt groggy and my leg was screaming in pain. I rolled over and was glad I fell asleep beside the river. Thank God. At least something was going right.

I pushed myself to my knees and crawled into the river. The water was like ice on the burn but seemed to heal a little of the pain. A twig snapped behind me. I grabbed my crossbow and an arrow and swung around, targeting the intruder; my heart stopped when I saw Chantelle.

I lowered my weapon and looked her over. She was covered in dirt and her jeans had rips all through them. I dropped my crossbow and ran to embrace her. She cried into my shoulder and held onto me like she was scared to let go.

'How'd you escape?' I asked, squirming out of her grip.

'They took me out of the cell. They said I was to be questioned, but I got away, and I just kept running.'

Her whole body was shaking with fear, I led her to the water and washed the dirt from her hands and face. It was unusual seeing her without make-up; she was always such a doll.

'Ariella,' someone called. I looked up but didn't recognise the man. 'I've been looking for you everywhere,' his eyes fell upon Chantelle. 'What are you doing with…'

'This is my friend Chantelle,' I interrupted. 'Do I know you?'

He looked hurt. 'It's me, Hale. When I came home you were gone.'

I tried to remember everyone I had met here. I had no recollection of being in his place. 'I'm sorry but I don't know who you are and I am very behind on my schedule so we must go.'

Chantelle took the lead as I took one last glance back at the man who claimed to know me. We walked through the forest for an hour. Darkness began to appear.

'I don't think this is the right way,' I said, stopping. 'You mustn't remember the way you escaped.'

'I do, it's just over this hill,' she said with confidence.

'Let's just rest for the night. You will remember better in the morning.'

As Chantelle sat resting with her back to a tree, I gathered sticks and rocks from the area. I placed the rocks in a circle to contain the fire and threw the sticks in the centre. I placed my hands over the sticks and close my eyes in hard concentration. *FIRE*, I willed silently. I opened my eyes but there was no flame. I closed my eyes, cleared my mind and tried again. Thirty minutes later we had a fire.

Chantelle fell asleep the moment the fire was blazing but my mind was too active to sleep. I held the locket within my fingertips. Such a small thing Jareth was willing to kill for. The moonstone in the centre of the pendant held such brilliance and energy that I wondered at the power it truly contained.

I hid the pendant beneath my weapons. I didn't like sleeping with it around my neck. I swore it had its own heartbeat. I laid beneath the stars and thought of home. I closed my eyes but didn't actually fall asleep. I heard a soft rustling and reached for my sword. I sat up and prepared an attack but froze when I saw Chantelle going through my things. It all made sense. She must have been freed in exchange for stealing the pendant.

'I almost wish I hadn't seen that,' I said softly. 'Is it just your freedom for the locket or the others as well?'

She laughed, a cold cruel laugh. 'It wasn't freedom you idiot. I've worked for Jareth longer than I've known you.'

CHAPTER TWENTY-THREE

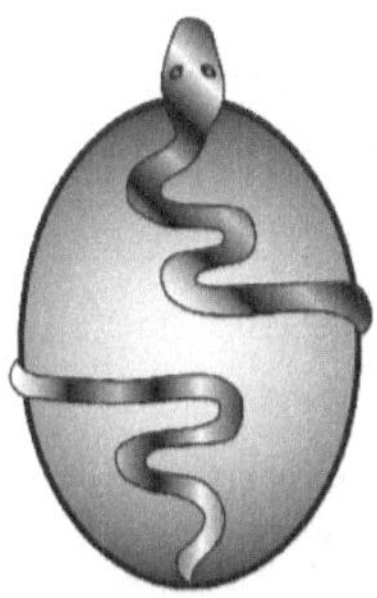

'How about I send you back to Jareth in a body bag as a message to stop screwing me around,' I snarled, anger welling up within me.

Chantelle ran off into the night without the locket. I quickly geared up again and put the locket safely around my neck to run after her. I followed her back to the waterfall. When I reached the water she had already climbed half way up the rocks.

'Why?' I yelled out. 'Were you my friend at all?'

She reached the top and looked back down at me. 'No, you annoying brat,' she yelled. 'I hated you and I hated that my mum got to play the fun taunting role.'

'Your mum?' I asked. 'I've never met your mum.'

'Jessica, you idiot,' she said, sounding annoyed. 'Haven't you worked out that we age differently to humans? Don't you ever wonder why Aurora looks to be in her twenties when she's meant to be your aunt?'

She turned around and ran off again. I splashed through the water to the falls and began to climb the rocks. I struggled not to fall but they were slippery from the water. I screamed in frustration as I finally reached the top. I ran over the wet rocks attempting to catch up to Chantelle again but my burnt leg was giving me grief. I kept running after Chantelle but I slipped and fell into a hole.

The first few moments I lay still on the ground I'd landed on. I took a second to catch my breath then pushed myself up. I couldn't see anything in this darkness so I put my hands out to find a wall. Finding it, I kept my hand running over it while I walked through the darkness. The rocky feel of the wall suddenly changed to smooth. I ran my hand over the smooth surface and felt that it was a door. I felt around until I found the knob and pulled it open.

I walked out and found myself back in the maze, though this section had a dark energy to it. A loud roar echoed around me and made the ground vibrate. Not waiting to find out what danger was coming from behind the maze walls, I ran as fast as my legs would carry me. My heart was pounding in my ears, and I only stopped when I came to a crossroad in the labyrinth.

'Ariella,' someone called out.

I turned around and saw a young brunette running towards me.

'Adriana, what are you doing here?' I asked as she reached me.

'You remember me?' she asked, seeming surprised.

I looked at her in confusion over her comment but I shrugged it off and asked her if her mother knew she was here. She looked at me with guilt all over her face; I groaned. Tatiana was going to be so angry with me.

'I couldn't tell her,' Adriana blurted out. 'She is under investigation from Jareth. He knows two women approached you; one of his spies told him. He has already worked out that it is most likely Yvette but he doesn't know who the second one is, so they are all under investigation.'

I apologised for the trouble I was putting her mother through and bid her goodbye, choosing a random path in the crossroad.

'You're going the wrong way,' Adriana called out. 'The castle is that way,' she said pointing in the opposite direction to the one I had decided to walk.

I rolled my eyes as we walked down the path she recommended. I smiled and laugh with ease as she told me stories about growing up with a strict mother, about sneaking out to flirt with boys and skipping school to spend the day lazing in a field, talking to animals. She reminded me of Serena. I teared up but blinked them away. I would find her. I would find and save all my friends.

We reached the end of the path which went down into a cave. Adriana smiled at me with big, child-like eyes full of excitement. She took my hand and led me into the cave. It was so dark that I could barely see her. I heard the sound of rushing water and saw a light in the distance.

The cave roof was suddenly metres high and we stood in a circular room with glowing vines falling from the ceiling, and a waterfall with glistening, crystal blue water. Adriana smiled at me before she ran into the water. She began to twirl, the water splashing at her knees. She signalled me in, her smile and excitement contagious. I walked towards her. The moment my foot entered the water I understood her happiness. The water made my skin tingle and spread a magical feeling through my entire being.

'What is this place?' I asked as we walked out of the water, and over to the other side of the cave.

'The cave of Freyja. She is a goddess from another world, but she fell in love with a warlock from here and this cave was their hideout. She is a deity of love.'

We walked the rest of the tunnel in silence. I kept replaying the feeling the water gave me. We finally entered sunlight and I blinked the view of the forest back into sight.

'How did Freyja's story end?' I asked, as we wandered through the trees.

'No one knows,' she said with a shrug. 'Most say that he disappeared and she moved on looking for her next love. Some say that they had a child who is now a queen of her own kingdom, but I don't think it was a happy ending.'

We settled down for the night. I let Adriana light the campfire, knowing she would be much quicker than me. I continued to think about the water in the cave. It had radiated so much happiness and positive energy. How did she not have a happy ending?

I heard a twig snap. I stood up, hand on the hilt of my sword. I turned and saw Adriana was standing up too, looking around, her sword already out and ready. A dozen men in black ski masks suddenly ran out of the trees and grabbed us. I didn't even have time to remove my sword from its scabbard. I struggled to look back and see Adriana. They had her pinned to the ground and were binding her hands. I yelled at them not to hurt her, but one of the men put a black bag over my head so I couldn't see anything. I struggled under their restraints as they forcefully walked me through the trees. I continually tripped over tree trunks, not being able to see where I was going. I heard Adriana snapping threats of what she was going to do to them when she escaped.

I was forced into a cart and my hands were bound behind my back, my legs tied to the chair. The bag was removed and I looked around for Adriana who was tied up next to me. The men were whispering in the corner and kept looking over at us. I looked to Adriana who was attempting to break free from her restraints.

A dark skinned man walked over and stood before me. His dark red eyes made him look terrifying. He opened up a book and flicked through the pages, saying nothing. He held his hand out and one of the other men ran over and handed him a jar of what looked like black sand. He began to walk in a circle around me, scattering the sand and muttering words in a language I didn't know or recognise.

'What are you doing?' I demanded, fear flooding my voice.

'A spell,' he said as he continued to walk around my chair. 'I've always wanted to perform it, I saw your father perform it on your mother but as you know that went horribly wrong.'

He stood before me, and started muttering unknown words again.

'What do you mean my father performed it on my mother?' I said. 'What spell are you doing?'

He sighed and glared at me. 'A power stripping spell. It weakened your mother so much that it killed her.'

As he started speaking the spell again, anger rose within me. My father stripped my mother of her powers and killed her! I glared at the book, willing it to be destroyed. The book suddenly lit up in flames, as well as the man reading the spell. I closed my eyes and turned away as he screamed in pain.

I felt my hands get cut free. I opened my eyes and Adriana was untying my ankle ropes. She pulled me up and we ran out of the room. I bent over and threw up when we were out of hearing range of screams. I did that, I killed him.

'Are you okay?' Adriana asked as she pulled my hair back and out of my face. I shook my head, guilty over what I just did. I didn't want that kind of magic. 'You can't feel bad about what you just did,' Adriana said. 'It wasn't a good thing, but you saved us and he was a bad guy.'

I straightened up and wiped my mouth. I thanked her for holding my hair back. We wandered back through the forest and back to our campsite. We reached it to find the fire was now nothing but burnt wood and ash. We lay beside it and attempted to get a few hours of sleep.

I was in a small dark room, my wrists in cuffs. I pulled on them and saw the chair I sat in was screwed into the floor. I leaned over and tried to pull myself free.

'Join the darkness,' echoed a cold, malicious voice.

I stood up and looked around, but I was completely alone. The voice spoke again, repeating the same sentence. I shook my head. I would not join the darkness. Water began to rise at my feet. Panicked, I leant forward again in an attempt to pull the chains free, but they wouldn't budge. The water continued to rise. I stood up, the water up to my neck. I tried to pull my hands out of the cuffs but they were on too tight. The water started to rise above my head. I coughed, water entered my lungs and I struggled to breathe. I felt a burn in my chest at the lack of oxygen in my lungs. I breathed in water one more time before waking up coughing, gasping for air.

I woke to Adriana leaning over me, looking pale as a sheet.

'I've been trying to wake you for like ten minutes.' She exhaled with relief. 'You weren't breathing and I couldn't wake you.'

I stood up, running my hands back through my hair. What was that?

'Which way to the castle?' I asked Adriana.

'Just keep going north,' she said.

I embraced her. 'Go home,' I told her. 'Don't argue with me. I just need to do this alone. I need to face him alone.'

She nodded, though I didn't believe she truly understood. I smiled at her then began walking north. The walk seemed much more tiring and quiet without company. I looked back and hoped that Adriana got home safely.

I walked north for what seemed like hours. I reached a dead end. Left or right? She hadn't told me this part; she had just said north. I looked around and saw Jace lying beneath a tree in the clearing to the left. I ran over to him and greeted him with a smile.

'Where have you been?' he asked.

'I don't even know,' I said, breathless. 'I keep ending up in different places.'

I looked past him at the tree. It was hollow. Within the tree was a passage way, and I was willing to bet it was the path to Jareth's castle. I walked past Jace and towards the hollow tree.

'Ariella,' he said.

I turned and looked at him. He was the first person to help me when I entered the maze.

'Don't go down there,' he said.

'Why not?' I asked. 'I asked you to take me to Jareth's castle and you knew this was the way the whole time. Were you going to show me?'

'You won't like what you find if you go down this path.'

'What aren't you telling me?' I asked.

He looked away from me for a second then looked back. 'Your mum gave her life to keep you out of this world. Remember that before you get yourself drawn too far in.'

I walked to the tree and saw a narrow staircase. I sighed deeply before I stepped into the tree and began my ascent up the stairs. This was the path that would lead me to the battle with my brother.

CHAPTER TWENTY-FOUR

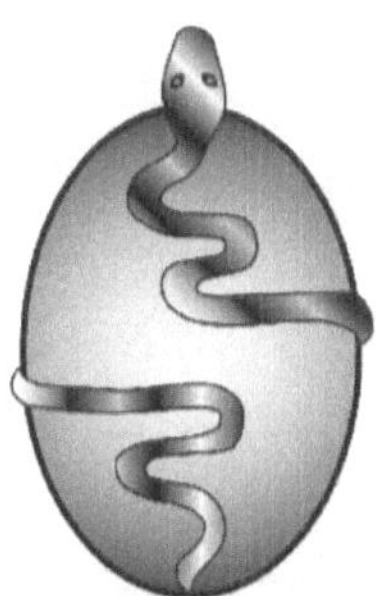

I found my way out onto a cliff overlooking a small valley, a forest and a clear path to the castle. The first thing to do was to somehow climb down this cliff. The rocks didn't look very secure.

I sat down and dangled my feet off the cliff. I turned onto my stomach and navigated my way down the cliff as carefully as possible and extremely slow. As my feet touched the ground I released a sigh of relief.

I took a step away from the cliff and looked down the next path I needed to take. I walked along a stone path through the trees until I entered into a valley. Two large rock walls lined a straight path to the castle. As I walked I tried to stay as close to one side of the wall as possible, feeling very vulnerable out in the open.

'Need help?' said a voice.

I jumped, magically making a rock explode beside where the voice came from. It was the young man from the waterfall. He looked from me to the...debris.

'I told you, I don't remember you,' I said angrily.

'I know,' he said sadly. 'But I knew your mother, and she'd want me to help you.'

'Chantelle was my friend for years and betrayed me. Why should I trust you?' I asked.

He looked me over. 'Your arm, I bound it for you.'

I looked at my injured arm and realised I didn't remember how it got bound. He walked over to me, hands up, kneeled down before me with a black cloth, like the one that already bound my arm and wrapped it around the burn on my leg. Then he stood up and took a step back again.

'Thank you,' I whispered.

I looked into the valley and saw what looked like a small wishing well. I walked over to it but before I could look inside the young man pulled me back.

'You may not like what you see,' he said.

'I don't even know who you are. Stop telling me what to do.'

'Zed Hale,' he said – déjà vu flickered within my mind.

'I need to see,' I said and looked into the water.

For a few moments all I saw was black water, but then Serena's face appeared. She was covered in dirt and coughing; she was in a dungeon. Jordan was there comforting her, his arms around her though he too looked to be shivering.

'Just hold in there Serena,' Eva said. She was sitting on the other side of Serena. 'Ariella will get us out of here.'

'I doubt that,' said a cold voice. Jareth stood at the bars, smiling maliciously at them. 'She won't make it to the castle alive.'

Jessica walked in and stood beside Jareth. 'My love, can I please torture the prisoners?' she said seductively, placing her hand on Jareth's arm.

He turned to her and kissed her deeply. 'Find Ariella first. Once she is gone they are all yours,' he said darkly and then walked away. She looked into the cage with a dark smile upon her lips.

'Surprise,' she said. 'Did you see this coming?'

'Yes because you're a cold hearted bitch,' Eva snapped back bravely.

'You're first little mouse,' she said spitefully. 'When I find your friend I am going to kill her and take the locket from her cold, dead body. And then

I am going to come back here, take you one by one and torture you all, slowly.'

'Back off Jessica,' said Jay. He sat huddled in the corner away from the others. 'Where'd you take my sister?'

'Your sister?' she laughed. 'We interrogated her, and when she wouldn't give us what we wanted to know, I had some fun with her.'

Jay was now at the gates trying to grab Jessica.

'You bitch,' he yells at her. 'Where is she?'

Jessica laughed. 'You'll see her again soon,' she whispered.

I looked away from the water. They didn't know that Chantelle was a traitor. How did Jay not know that Jessica and Chantelle were both in league with Jareth? And Jessica, she was the female voice that was pursuing me. I knew I recognised her voice.

'What'd you see?' Hale asked as I walked away from the wishing well and continued down the valley.

'The people I am trying to save.'

CHAPTER TWENTY-FIVE

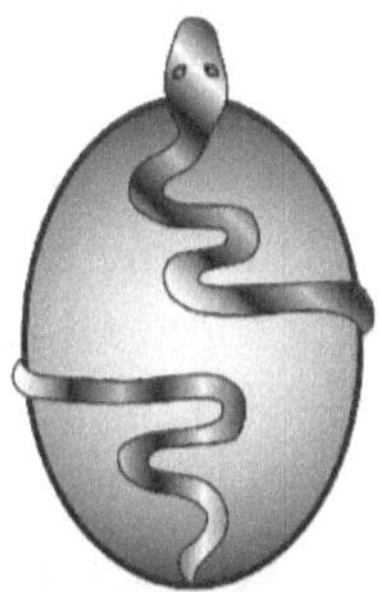

He ran up and fell into step beside me. 'Do you know how to use those weapons you carry?' he asked.

'I've read about using them,' I replied bluntly.

He grabbed my arm. 'I'll train you, before it gets too dark.'

I nodded. He walked over to the edge of the valley and picked up a red rock. He drew a small red circle onto the valley wall. He walked back to me then went over to the other side of the valley. I could barely see the red circle he drew.

'Try and shoot it,' he said, pointing to the red circle.

I looked at him thinking he was joking, but the look in his eyes held seriousness and faith. I took out my bow and an arrow. I aimed, took a deep breath and released the arrow. It didn't even hit the wall. It hit the ground a few feet in front of me.

I awkwardly looked away.

'Set it up again' he said.

I retrieved another arrow and prepared the shot. He stood behind me, lowered my elbow and moved my hand so the tip of the arrow's feather was touching my lips.

'Aim and don't breathe,' he whispered in my ear. I did as he said. This time my arrow still didn't hit the target but I hit the wall at least. I smiled at him and felt a familiar flutter in my stomach when he smiled back.

He walked over to the wall retrieving the arrows I just shot. I was silently hoping we kept practising because the simplest touch between us made my skin feel as though it was on fire.

'We'll reuse these arrows,' he said as though reading my mind. 'We don't want to make all your tips blunt.'

He handed me one of the arrows he just retrieved.

'Thanks,' I whispered as I took it.

I prepared another shot, remembering what he said. I released and again I hit the wall but not the target. For over an hour it continued like this. I stretched my arms which were sore and tired, and looked over at Hale where he had been leaning against a rock for the last half an hour to see he was asleep. I was a little offended but then again if I was watching someone do this for an hour I would have fallen asleep too. Okay, just one more try and I'd call it for the day. I loaded an arrow and drew my arm back. I took a deep breath then aimed and released. I screamed in excitement when my arrow finally hit the red circle. Hale jerked awake from the sound. When he noticed I was screaming in excitement and not fear he stood up and walked over to me.

'Knew you could do it,' he said with a smile I wanted to melt in.

'Now the knife,' he said.

I pulled it out and looked at him for instruction.

'Hold it defensively,' he said.

I had no idea what he meant so I just held it forward. He smiled in amusement. Hale positioned my arms as though I was in a boxing match, the knife uncomfortably close to my face. He held his arms out for me to attack. I swung knowing he was going to move out of the way but I found the movement easy.

As night fell I found myself comfortable with the knife and a good aim with a bow, though I was yet to practise on a moving target.

'Tell me about the first time we met,' I asked Hale as we sat around a small fire.

He looked at me across the flames, a sad smile playing upon his lips. 'You found me in the rainforest meadow. I bound your arm and hid you from the guards. I volunteered to help you and took you to a safe place to rest.'

'What aren't you telling me?' I asked.

He hesitated for a moment., 'You kissed me,' he said softly.

I nodded but didn't say anything. I stood up and walked around the fire and knelt before him. I pressed my lips to his, his hand brushing through my hair. Blurred images of our first kiss in the hollow tree seeped back into my memory along with multiple other memories: everything I'd lost in that cursed place Jareth had sent me to was back, and so was the memory that Hale was engaged.

'I remember,' I whispered.

He leant forward and kissed me again. 'Remember what?' he asked.

'The meadow and our first kiss in that tree,' I whispered.

'The first male suitor to kiss you since you entered Alesmera and your last I hope,' he said.

'Right,' I said faking a smile. Julius was actually my first kiss and what a kiss that was.

I lay beside Hale and looked up at the stars. I wanted to tell him that I remembered he had a fiancée but I needed him to get me to the castle first. I knew that sounded horrible but I'd left my friends there for far too long.

'Tell me about your childhood,' I said, trying to subtly move over a little bit.

'I grew up in the rainforest,' he said, gazing up at the stars. 'Mum wasn't a well-known accomplice of your mum but a few people did know so we didn't want to set up in Jareth's kingdom. We thought you were lost and I was glad, because I knew your mum had hidden you for a reason. I was so angry at Mum when she said Yvette had found you and that she was going to reveal the truth, but now I am glad you came back.'

'What do you mean, came back?' I asked. 'I've never been here before.'

'Yes you have,' he whispered, brushing a loose strand of hair back from my face. 'You were born here. Aurora took you to the human world after your mother died.'

I fell asleep under the stars and in front of the fire's warmth. I started thinking that if it wasn't for my friends being kidnapped or traitors, a locket that could destroy the world or my psychotic half-brother, I would feel at home here, finally after all these years.

Upon waking we jumped straight into sword practise. I dropped the sword after a few minutes because it was so heavy and my arms were so sore from yesterday. Hale walked up to me and kissed me. For a second I melted into his kiss but then I remembered that he had a fiancée. I pushed away from him.

'You can't kiss me Hale,' I said, not meeting his gaze.

'What do you. . .' he started to ask me. 'You remember.'

I nodded.

'About that. . .' he started to say but I held my hand up.

'Please,' I interrupted before he can start talking again. 'I don't want to talk right now; I just need to save my friends. We can talk later.'

He nodded and told me to pick my sword back up. He decided until I got the feel of it I should start with just drawing my sword. You'd think it'd be easy, but I kept pulling out my sword and immediately dropping it.

'You have to have a firm grip before you pull it out,' Hale said as he demonstrated drawing his sword. 'You have to take a strong grasp, draw it out as quickly as possible and then positon yourself ready for a fight.'

'I'm trying,' I snapped. 'I didn't grow up in fairy-tale land.'

His eyes softened. 'I'm sorry if I'm being harsh Ariella. I'm just trying to help you.'

'I know. I'm just tired and still adjusting to everything. I mean a few days ago I was just a normal teenager in high school.'

'You're a quick learner. You're doing amazing. Let's move on.'

I lost my balance and landed on my butt for the tenth time. 'Remember to step. You're letting your feet get too close together and then you lose balance.'

'I'm going to hurt tomorrow aren't I? My arms are already dead from yesterday's bow and knife training,' I complained.

'Your body will get used to it and stop hurting...eventually,' he said.

As I blocked Hale's attacks I noticed that if I watched his shoulders rather than his sword I could disarm him quicker. I also had to focus on keeping the sword close to my body and not swinging it away wildly.

There was so much to remember, but I was a natural and picking up tricks quickly. It was hard keeping distance between Hale and I in our practise fights since I wasn't fast enough to step back when he went in for an attack. To avoid a fatal blow, I had to keep the distance of his sword between us.

As the hours went by I found myself getting faster and having better footing. Unfortunately knowing your surroundings was also a key to winning so Jareth would have one up on me, but I could do it, because I had a cause and motivation. I just hoped that it was enough.

I heard a twig snap and turned to the sound. I saw Chantelle making her way through the valley. Anger welled up in me and I ran after her. I heard Hale screaming my name but I didn't stop. I heard a creature roar above me and then something knocked me off my feet. I looked up and saw the strangest creature. It had a lion's head, a goat's body and a dragon's tail.

'Chimaera,' I heard Hale yell. 'Run!'

I saw Chantelle running for cover, her face full of fear. She peered out of her hiding place and smiled at me. Anger boiled within me and I felt my magic beneath my skin.

I held my hand up and whispered, 'Give me flame.'

A fire ball appeared in my hand and I threw it at the creature. It was merely a momentary distraction for me to run past it and after Chantelle who had started running again. I could hear the creature behind me but too much was resting on me getting to that castle. Encouraged by that thought I pushed my body to run faster.

Chantelle was running too fast for me to catch up, so I stopped in my tracks and I grabbed my bow and arrow. Jumping onto a high rock, I took aim, remembering what Hale had taught me: feather upon my lip and elbow down. I released the arrow and watched it soar though the air. Chantelle fell to the ground. Before I could jump off the rock I was thrown from it. I rolled over as the Chimera flew towards me. Pulling out another arrow I aimed it at the creature's heart. I hit its shoulder instead, which slowed it down momentarily. I got up and started running again. As I reached Chantelle I spun on my heel and drew another arrow. I aimed again for the creature's heart but hit its leg, and like the first hit it only slowed down the creature. I needed to get on higher ground for a better shot. Suddenly I wished I'd somehow been able to practise on a moving target.

A flame appeared in from of me. I grabbed it and it turned to paper. I quickly opened it. It read two words: Bronze Blade

I pulled my blade from my belt and whispered the words repeatedly, 'Turn to bronze, turn to bronze.'

Nothing. 'Dammit,' I cursed.

I retrieved another arrow and took aim, noticing that my arrow tip had changed from silver to bronze. I lowered the bow and retrieved the arrow to get a better look at the tip. It had turned to bronze. I did it. I looked up and saw the Chimera was now on foot and running towards me. I took a step back and fell backwards, throwing my bow. I pushed myself up, still holding the arrow.

The Chimera tackled me and pinned me to the ground and with no other weapon in my hand I pushed the arrowhead up and the force of the creature pouncing on me pushed the tip into its heart. It let out a horrible roar and collapsed beside me. I lay there paralysed, my heart racing. I took deep breaths to calm myself down. The shock was over. I rolled over and pushed myself up off the ground, walking over to Chantelle who was still grounded from my arrow which hit her in the thigh.

I stood before Chantelle looking down at her. She began to laugh.

'What are you laughing at?' I snapped.

'You,' she said, pushing herself to her feet, supporting her leg. 'You're looking all grown up compared to that innocent little book geek in school.'

I slapped her. 'You're a bitch,' I snarled. 'Do you even care that your brother thinks you're dead and is going mad with rage? That Serena, Jordan and Eva are rotting in a cage? Is there any remorse in that heartless body?' I yelled.

'No,' she snarled back, then before I saw it coming she pulled a knife out and jammed it into my stomach.

I fell to my knees, my hand holding the knife still.

I looked at her. 'I loved you'

I saw a flicker of emotion in her eyes, but it was gone too quick for me to be sure.

'You cried in primary school when your brother wouldn't pass you the ball in football,' I said, tears threatening my eyes. 'In eighth grade, for a whole week, you would sneak in my window and come sleep in my bed because you couldn't sleep. We would stay up for hours talking and counting the stars on my roof, you told me. You did love me at one stage.'

Chantelle scoffed and me, and laughed at me like I was being weak.

'I remember, the first night you snuck through my window, you told me your mother told you something that made you angry and want to hate her. I told you that it doesn't matter if it makes you angry, she's your mum, and you have to make her proud.'

Chantelle slapped me this time. 'How do you know that Jay, Serena, Jordan or Eva even care about you? If I managed to fake it they could have been too,' she snapped before limping off.

CHAPTER TWENTY-SIX

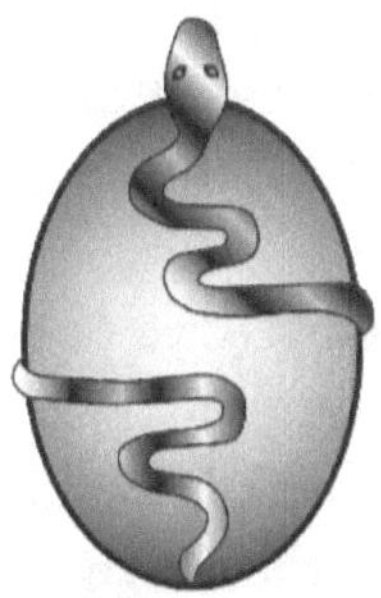

'Hale,' I shrieked before falling onto my back. I heard him scream my name before I saw him reach me. He took his jacket off and rolled it into a pillow, putting it under my head. As Hale cleaned my wound with water I couldn't stop the screaming in my head. It hurt so much.

'I don't know what else to do,' Hale said in a panic. 'There are no healing herbs in this area of the land.'

'Move over,' said a voice. I looked up and saw Arya.

She was…naked.

Was I seeing this right? Perhaps I was delirious or lost more blood than I realised? A stab wound would lose a lot of blood, wouldn't it? I blinked and looked up again. She was definitely naked, well, almost. She was wearing a black bra and underwear with knee high boots, a weapons belt and bow and arrow harnessed to her back.

Hale went to argue but when he saw her he obediently stepped aside. Did he know her or did he obey because she was pretty much naked and gorgeous and everything I wasn't? She bent down over me and pulled out two sachets.

She handed Hale one of them and said, 'Crush this within water. Its Gotu Kola. It'll speed up the healing process.'

As he went to work Arya pulled off the cloth on my arm and leg and opened a second sachet pulling out a spiky leaf. It was thick and when she snapped it in half. I saw what looked like some form of gel. She spread it over the cut on my arm and the burn on my leg.

'It's Aloe Vera,' she said as she rewrapped the cloth.

'You're not meant to be here,' I whispered, remembering what she said to me before I embarked on this seemingly crazy journey.

'I sensed your pain. You needed medical help,' she said softly, taking her kindness to a level I hadn't predicted.

'Why are you almost naked?' I asked.

She smiled as though she had momentarily forgotten. 'You've seen me in just a towel and you didn't ask me then.'

I laughed.

Her face turned serious. 'Haven't you wondered why Jareth hasn't bothered you or set anymore traps the past few hours? I was keeping him busy and I couldn't find my clothes when I sensed your pain.'

'Jareth, really?' was all I could muster.

She shrugged. 'He wasn't always bad,' she said. 'His mother was kind and when he lived with her, he was too. It's all Aubrey's influence now.'

'But the Chimera attacked us,' I wondered out loud.

'It's not the only thing that guards the valley from unwanted guests,' Arya explained.

'Ready,' Hale said offering the bowl to her.

She grabbed my knife. 'Silver? Did you not get my fire message?'

'I did,' I reply. 'I accidently turned an arrowhead bronze instead.'

Without hesitation she put her hand over the bowl and cut across her palm. She showed no outward sign of pain. I watched her blood drip into the bowl.

'Mix,' she said to Hale, now binding her own hand after placing the Aloe Vera on it.

She took the bowl from Hale and picked out some of the crushed green leaves placing them on my knife wound. I cried out in pain.

'Sorry,' she whispered. She turned to Hale. 'Make sure she is rested. Reapply tonight and tomorrow morning – there is to be no movement until midday tomorrow at the earliest. Do you understand?'

Hale nodded and took the bowl back.

'Don't leave,' I said as Arya stands up.

'I must. When I sensed your pain I kind of snuck out of Jareth's chambers. He'll have noticed I have left by now. I must leave.' She smiled at me then walked away.

Hale sat beside me. 'You'll be okay,' he whispered.

'Ariella,' called out a voice, but I was too weak to sit up and see who it was.

Jace ran into view.

'Her Majesty told me to come help keep guard for the night,' he said as I looked at him with confusion.

'Who is Her Majesty?' I asked, sick and tired of not being in the loop.

'Miss Arya,' he said, seemingly puzzled that I didn't know.

'Are you serious?' I blurted out.

In all this time she had been helping me take back my kingdom. Why wasn't she fighting for hers?

As night fell Hale reapplied some more leaves and I fell asleep with both Jace and Hale on night watch.

CHAPTER TWENTY-SEVEN

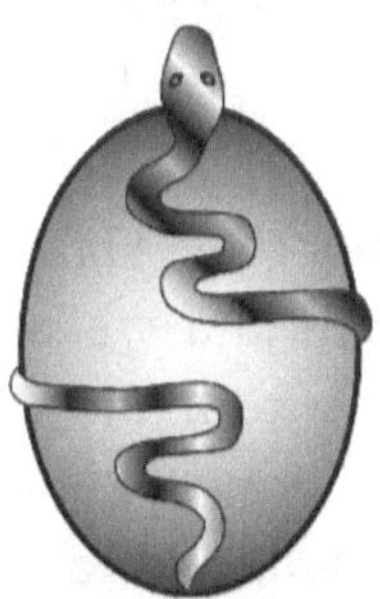

It had been twenty-four hours since Chantelle stabbed me and I was now ridiculously restless. My injuries weren't perfectly healed but they were good enough for me to go on.

'Chantelle is getting away,' I argued when Hale and Jace protested that I needed more rest.

'You can't go after her,' Hale demanded. 'You can't be angry with her when you face her.'

I scoffed. 'What does that have to do with anything?'

'Because of your curse,' he said. 'You're born of the purest good and the worst evil in Alesmera which means you can access both dark and light magic, so if you access magic in anger you risk being consumed by dark magic.'

'I don't believe you,' I snapped back.

I reassembled all my weapons and started walking down the valley. I needed to catch up to Chantelle. Hale ran up to me and grabbed my wrist. I shot him a dark look and zapped him like I had to Jessica in school.

'Chantelle and Jessica are going to torture and kill me and everyone I love, so either help me defeat them or let me go,' I fumed trying to pull free of his grasp.

Jace ran up and took Hale's hand off me. I looked at them both and walked off not looking back. I thought of Aurora and wondered how she was feeling right now. I thought of Serena coughing in that small, cold cage.

I found a blood trail but it was hard to follow over the rocky terrain. I had my bow and arrow ready in hand as I follow the blood drops. I wouldn't be surprised by anything.

I heard a small cry. Hiding behind the rock I was currently approaching I peered around it. Chantelle sat beside a small creek washing the wound I gave her. A giant roar echoed from the skies. I prayed it wasn't another Chimera. As I stepped out from the rock I heard it again. Staring up at the valley opening I saw a copper and black dragon. It landed before Chantelle and roared again. She screamed and got up to run but it blew fire at her which she only just managed to dodge.

'Jareth,' she screamed, as though he'd hear her. 'Call off your pet.'

It blew another flame at her which she scarcely escaped. She pulled herself to her feet but stumbled back to the ground as the dragon advanced on her.

I jumped out from my hiding place and shot an arrow where its heart should have been but the arrow didn't even dent its scale. Unfortunately, now its attention was on me. I ran to Chantelle and pulled her to her feet.

'Run,' I yelled.

'Why are you helping me?' she asked as we ran.

'Because I want to kill you myself,' I snapped.

The dragon landed in front of us and we both threw ourselves to the ground as it breathed another flame. I rolled onto my back and grabbed my knife. I closed my eyes and whispered *bronze blade*. I opened my eyes and smiled when I saw it had worked. I threw it at the dragon's hide and exhaled in relief when I saw it break the scale from the dragon's hide, but it didn't penetrate the skin. It spat more fire at us which hit Chantelle's arm. She screamed in pain and fell to the ground. The dragon rose into the air and circled us.

'Jareth you coward,' I yelled. 'Your girlfriend is out here dying and you sit in your castle! Why don't you come save her life you jerk?'

I ran over to Chantelle and helped her to her feet. 'How do you defeat a dragon?' I asked as I dragged her down the valley.

'Dragons are secretive,' she complained.

'That's not helping,' I argued.

'The elements,' she said.

'What? Isn't that Earth, Water. . .'

'Wind and Fire,' she finished.

The dragon was preparing to land again. I put Chantelle down and focused on the liquid in the air but I couldn't feel more than a splash of water in this place. I cursed under my breath and reloaded my bow again.

'Give me ice,' I breathed and watched as the tip of my arrow turned to ice. I released the arrow which broke off another scale.

It roared in anger and then flew out of the valley and out of sight.

'Did you get it?' Chantelle asked.

'Yes,' I lied.

'You know I am still going to torture your little friends,' she snarled.

The anger I'd forgotten bubbled inside me and I focused it on her. She began coughing like she couldn't breathe. I could hear yelling from behind me but I felt as though I was in a trance. I could feel Chantelle's life force...feel it fading. I was suddenly thrown back and hit the ground hard.

When I looked up I saw Hale standing over Chantelle.

'You almost killed her,' he yelled at me. 'I warned you about the dark magic.'

'I had it under control,' I snapped as I stumbled onto my feet. 'You used magic on me.'

'I had no choice,' he argued.

'Whatever,' I mumbled under my breath. 'I have to get to the castle.'

'What about her?' he asked.

'I won't kill her, but I'm not helping her either, because I tried to. I protected her from the dragon and she still vowed to kill my friends – now let's go, the dragon is going to come back soon.'

'You said you got it,' Chantelle yelled at me.

I shrugged. 'I lied.'

Hale looked from me to her and then followed me down the last stretch to the castle.

We reached the forest. Though it didn't look like a normal forest: the trees were black – the trunks, the leaves, the thorns – darker than night.

'The dark forest,' Hale told me. 'It hides the castle from intruders; for guests he wants, it shows a path through the darkness.'

'We aren't going to get a yellow brick road.'

He looks at me with confusion.

'It's from this book Aurora bought me from a shop called "Outer Realm". Their store motto is that every item they sell is from another universe. I used to think it was just a sales pitch but if magic places like this exist I suppose other realms can too. Anyways it's this story about this girl that finds a magic world through a tornado she and her house get sucked up into and she has to follow a yellow brick road to get to the emerald city.' Yes, I was rambling, just to myself, entering the forest.

'Want me to go first?' Hale asked, guessing why I was rambling.

I shook my head. This was my mission; I needed to take the lead. I walked into the dark forest looking for the secret path. Instead I found I couldn't see. It was pitch black and it was near impossible for me to see the outline of the trees. As I continued to walk I finally saw the faintest light in the distance. I was almost there. I turned to tell Hale but found myself alone. I called out to him but no sound left my mouth. I side stepped to turn around and look for him but I lost my balance and fell into a lake. *Please be no creatures in here,* I prayed to myself as I stood up. I noticed at that point that the lake was too thick to be water. I quickly dragged myself back onto the bank and ran for the light. When I escaped the forest I looked down at myself and screamed. I was covered in blood.

'Will you shut up?' said a cold voice. I looked up and saw Jessica walking towards me. 'I see you found our river of blood. It's a nice touch don't you think?'

Glancing around, I quickly took in my surroundings, my bow still in my hands. I pulled out an arrow and released it at Jessica. It was a perfect shot. Well, it would have been if she hadn't caught it. She laughed more maliciously than I'd ever heard. With a sinister look back at me she snapped the arrow in half.

'Sweetheart, just because I look sixteen, doesn't mean I am,' she said. 'If I was going to let you live I would say read up on your history. How is it that you know nothing about your heritage?'

'How old is Aurora?' I asked, curiosity taking over.

'The little Atlanta sister?' Jessica questioned. 'She would be eighty, close to ninety and your mother would be over a hundred if she were still alive, but never mind that naïve bitch; your father is the true talent. He was amazing in the war. It's just a shame that Jareth was too young to fight. He would have been magnificent to watch.'

'What war?' I needed to keep asking her questions to keep her distracted. Hale was going to emerge behind me any second now. I could feel it.

'It happened just over twenty years before you were born,' she replied fondly. 'If I get my timeline right, I spent too much time in the human world keeping an eye on you. If you had stayed inactive we would have left you alone.'

'Which side did you fight for?'

She eyes me suspiciously. 'We were technically fighting for your side, because the other side was led by a Spider Demon. Horrible creatures. But enough of this history lesson. Draw your sword. I'd hate to kill you when you were defenceless.'

Each lesson Hale gave me went through my mind as my sword clashed against Jessica's. As she went for a killing blow I threw myself to the ground and kicked my leg out to knock her back. Before she had a chance to get back up I grabbed her sword and threw it as hard as I could. Then I pinned her to the ground with an arrow aimed at her throat.

'Where is he keeping them?'

'Dungeon,' she snarled.

I pulled her to her feet and pushed her against the tree, binding her hands behind it in a constrictor knot with my belt. It was a relatively simple and easy knot to tie but near impossible to untie, especially from behind your own back.

'You're not just going to leave me here are you?' she argued.

I smiled at her, remembering all the school drama I went through with her. 'I am sure someone will find you eventually.'

CHAPTER TWENTY-EIGHT

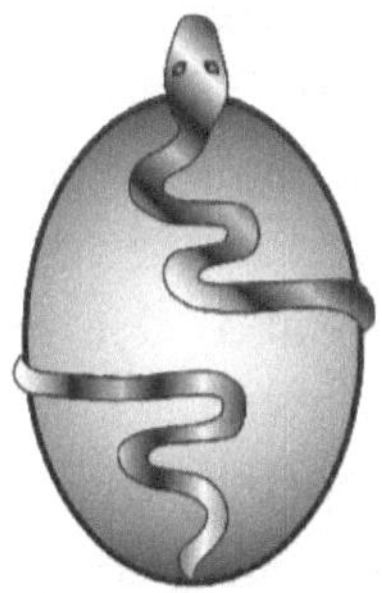

As I first entered the castle I was surprised with its lack of security. I suppose most people wouldn't survive the Chimera, the dragon, the black forest and Jessica. I was actually impressed with myself.

There was a staircase to the left which led downstairs. I figured that was my best bet to find the dungeon. I mean they were always at the very bottom room in the furthest chamber of the castle, right?

I edged silently though the hallways, hiding whenever I heard footsteps. Sighing in frustration, I realised I was getting nowhere. I heard voices up ahead so I slipped through the nearest door. It was a bedroom and was very dusty, as though it hadn't been used in a long while. Above the bed was a large portrait of my mother – she was smiling and sitting on a staircase in a red ball gown. I walked over to the bed and picked up a small frame that sat on the bedside table – it was my mother holding me as a baby.

I realised that this must have be my parents' old room, when they had been happy. I put the frame back down and walked to the door. I looked back at the photo of my mother and felt an ache in my chest. I pulled the door open and stepped out into the hallway. I heard someone shout. I looked up to see a guard running towards me. I drew my knife and slashed his hand. He was momentarily distracted so I ran down the hall. Regrettably I was still a klutz and tripped down the stairs.

Before I had a chance to get up two guards pulled me to my feet and dragged me downstairs…to the dungeon. Well at least I knew where it was now. They threw me into an empty cell and I noticed straight away that my friends were in the cell beside me.

'Eva,' I screeched running to the bars. She turned around and ran to me. We hugged through the bars. I looked around her and saw Jordan smiling warily at me. Serena seemed to be unconscious.

'Is she okay?' I asked.

He shook his head.

'Did you see Chantelle?' Eva asked hopefully. I peered over to Jay who looked to doze off.

'She and Jessica were in league with Jareth this whole time,' I whispered, looking down at the ground as I spoke.

'She couldn't be,' Eva argued. 'Chantelle is our friend.'

I shook my head and she looked at me sadly and then over to Jordan who was now awake and looking betrayed.

We sat in silence for what felt like hours and then I heard the guards whispering. I stood up and walked to the front of the cell so I could hear better.

'He is on the move,' the guard whispered.

'Are you sure?' urged the other. 'Well that would explain why Jareth is so stressed.'

'Does Aubrey know that he lost the pendant?'

'Jareth hasn't returned any of his fire messages since it happened, but the last one said he is returning to Alesmera.'

I turned around and walked to the centre of my cell; my father was coming. I felt like I was being sucked into a whirlwind of emotions. I was anxious to meet my father for the first time. I felt guilty for feeling anxious after what he did to my mother, angry for him hurting and betraying her. But above all I was nervous that he wouldn't even give me a second glance and side with Jareth. I felt numb.

I turned around to face the gates. Holding my hands in a fist at my chest I focused on the bars. I thrust my arms forward and opened my hands, a small, silent explosion denting one of the bars. I kept repeating the movement and focusing on each emotion until there was a hole big enough for me to slip through.

'Our turn now,' I heard Jay say. I looked at him, and I realised I didn't trust him.

'Where were you born?' I asked.

He looked at me confused. 'Mystic, just like you.'

'How is it Jessica and Chantelle are in league with Jareth and you didn't know anything about it?'

'What are you going on about? Chantelle isn't in league with him,' he argued.

'Let's play a game,' I said slyly. He looked at me as though we were wasting escape time. 'I am going to say a word, and you say the first word that comes to your head, got it?'

It wasn't an original idea but it was a game that generally proved to be effective.

'This is a waste of time,' he snapped.

'Sky,' I said, ignoring him.

'Blue.'

'Tree.'

'Tall.'

'School.'

'Stupid.'

'Sports.'

'Fun.'

'Jareth.'

'Lord.'

I smiled. He realised what he'd done and went to grab Eva. I screamed out NO and flung out my hand which threw a wave of energy at Jay and knocked him out cold. I heard the guards running down the stairs; I jumped out of my cage and quickly grabbed my bow which was hanging on the wall. I snatched two arrows from the quiver and shot both guards in their legs. They collapsed to the ground.

'If you make a noise I will shoot you in the other leg,' I said warningly. 'Keys?'

The first one I hit handed them to me. He looked at me, puzzled. 'Why didn't you just kill us?' he asked as he held his leg.

'You're just following orders,' I said.

I turned to unlock the cage. Eva and Jordan carried Serena out.

'Get in the cage,' I said to the guard. The second guard stood and went to attack me but the first one, who gave me the keys, stopped him.

'You'll make a better leader than Jareth' he said as he unarmed the second guard and dragged him into the cell.

I locked it and handed the first guard back his sword. 'Just in case you have trouble with them two,' I whispered. 'I'll come back when I've dealt with my brother.'

CHAPTER TWENTY-NINE

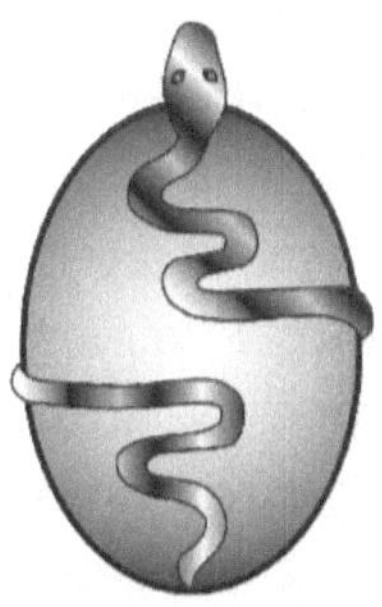

We walked back along the path I was dragged down until we reached the staircase. I search for guards and signalled the others to follow me as I walked silently up the staircase. I needed to get Serena out of the castle, then I would go and find Jareth. I found my way back to the hall and sighed in annoyance. It was now swarming with guards. You would have thought it would be harder to break into a castle than out of one. I saw Hale on the other side of the hall. I signalled to him that I had the others; he winked at me then jumped out of his hiding place.

'Excuse me, guards.' They all turned to look at him. 'There is a girl in the dark forest that highly resembles the girl that our Lord is hunting.'

'Thank you Sir,' they replied as they ran out to attack, well, me.

Hale ran over to me once the hall was cleared out. He took in the sight of Jordan and Eva carrying Serena. He took Serena into his arms as though she was weightless.

'Be careful. Win. And meet back at mine. Do you remember how to get back?'

I nodded. He signalled to Eva and Jordan to follow him and I watched them run outside and away from the castle.

The hall led to a set of large red doors above a grand staircase which I was willing to bet would lead me to the throne. I glanced out the doors to see the guards were surrounding the dark forest.

This was it. I ran towards the staircase; I heard no one follow me which I took as a good sign. As I went up the stairs I felt as though I was ascending into my strength, into my role, into my destiny.

In one motion I pushed open the doors and walked inside the throne room, closing the doors behind me. Jareth sat in the large chair at the end of the room, smiling at me.

'Surprised?' I asked as I walked towards him.

'Very.' He stood up. 'You, a girl with no magical training or talent managed to fight her way through my valley of traps with barely a scratch.'

I bowed sarcastically and rather overdramatically. 'I guess we really are related.'

He laughed. 'You can't beat me,' he bragged. 'I am stronger than you in magic, mind and strength.'

'Who makes it has no need of it, who buys it have no use for it, who uses it can neither see nor feel it. What is it?' I asked, still walking towards him.

'Is this how you're going to play?' he asked, sitting back down in his chair. He muttered the riddle back to himself. 'A coffin – what is greater than god, more evil than the devil, the poor have it, the rich need it, and if you eat it, you'll die?'

'Nothing,' I guessed.

'You may believe you can beat me mentally but how about with a sword?' He stood up and drew his blade.

I drew my sword and held it before me, protecting myself. I watched his shoulders, waiting for him to strike.

He swung first, hitting my sword with such force I lost my stability for a moment. I balanced my footing and swung my sword at him, hitting his arm. It seemed to impress him. He waved his hand throwing me back into the wall. When I hit the floor I coughed up blood.

Reaching for my sword I stood before him again. I kept blocking his blows but I knew I had to get out of defence sooner rather than later. As he gave me an opening I swung a fatal blow but he waved his hand again and threw me back into the wall. My vision blacked out for just a second.

In my moment of unconsciousness, I heard my mother's voice in my head. *'Fight my darling, fight for me – stay alive.'*

I looked up at Jareth's cold malicious eyes; his lips had a spiteful smirk upon them. I pushed myself up from the ground and recovered my sword. Jareth swung a deadly blow which I scarcely dodged. I spun around and my blade collided with his cheek.

'You can't beat me sister. You don't have the power.'

I swung my blade to clash with his and I looked deep into his piercing eyes that held such confidence. Focusing all my energy on the surroundings around me I felt the ground begin to shake; Jareth's confidence faltered for a moment.

'Careful sister, you'll destroy us both,' he snarled as a vortex of bright light opened up behind him.

'I...AM...NOT...YOUR...SISTER,' I yelled, then turned around and kicked him in the chest throwing him back into the vortex. Just before he was flung back I felt a tug at my neck. Jareth laughed as he disappeared into oblivion, making a chill go down my spine. My hand went to where the pendant had sat at my throat to find it missing. That was why he was laughing. He got the pendant back.

CHAPTER THIRTY

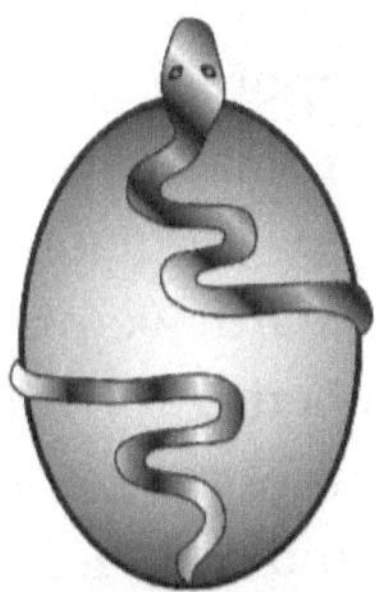

The pendant was lost but so was Jareth so I felt as though I'd won. The kingdom was mine. I sent a fire letter to Hale telling him I won, that I was okay and I would return to the meadow as soon as possible.

I went back to the dungeon and let the guard who had helped me out. He bowed to me.

'I am Colt. I am in debt and loyal to your rule.'

'I promote you to the head of my security,' I said handing him the cell keys. 'I want you to find

Chantelle and Jessica and sort through the guards that are willing to work with me over the ones who are loyal to Jareth. The cage is big enough for all against me.'

I returned to the hall to find Yvette and Tatiana waiting for me. Yvette ran to me and embraced me.

'I knew you could do it, Your Highness,' she said with a small bow.

Tatiana took me aside. 'Zed loves you.' I laughed to cover my scoff. 'He left her for you. He called off the engagement.'

I looked at her and saw no lie in her eyes. I wanted to run to Hale but no, not yet, he could wait a day or two. I smiled in spite of myself.

I left Colt in temporary charge and journeyed home to Aurora. Yvette gave me a charm that transported me to the mortal world. The ingredients for the charm were difficult to come by but she had a few left. As I walked through the doors of my human home the first thing Aurora did was run to me and embrace me. I realised how much I had missed her. We sat on the couch and I told her everything. She laughed in all the parts that Arya was in and I noticed her tense every time I talked about the Hale parts. I didn't tell her about Julius. I'm not sure why, but for some reason I kept him a secret.

'It sounds like you found out who you really are,' she said to me with a small smile. 'Now I have something to tell you.'

I looked at her curiously and she held up her left hand which now had a large diamond upon it. I let out a scream of excitement and hugged her. I knew William was the one.

As much as I wanted to stay and continue to catch up with Aurora I had too much else to do so I said my goodbyes and promised to visit properly once all was in order. I re-entered Alesmera through Styr's realm as Arya taught me.

'Your Highness,' he said as he saw me. 'Your power grows. Learn to control it before it controls you,' he warned.

'What happens if it controls me?' I asked.

He looked sad for a moment. 'Ask Arya.'

I remembered the look of hunger she got when she used minimum magic. That's why she had used herbs to heal me instead of magic. She was afraid of it taking control over of her again. If someone as amazing as her could lose control, how easy would it be for me I wondered.

'Your mother is proud of you,' he said as I opened the door to the maze.

I looked at him over my shoulder. 'How do you know?' I asked.

'Because I can commune with the dead,' he said. 'I'm not just a gate keeper to the living. She saw you, kept an eye on you and she wanted me to tell you she loves you and whatever you hear it's not your fault.'

I turned around to face him. 'What does that mean?'

He shook his head. 'I cannot say Your Highness.'

I nodded, accepting his answer, and walked out the door back to my home, Alesmera. I walked down into the forest area of the realm and found Hale waiting for me at his front door. I smiled and hugged him when I reached him.

'I'm glad you survived,' he whispered.

'How are they?' I asked. I'd left my friends in his care. I walked inside and see Jordan and Eva at the table eating. They looked much healthier. I smiled at them as I walked past and into the bedroom where Serena lay. She smiled at me as I entered.

'You look much better,' I said as I lay on the bed beside her.

'I feel much better,' she whispered. 'You did it; I knew you would.'

I played with a strand of her hair and watched her fall back to sleep. Leaving the bedroom, I went back to the front door where Hale was still standing.

'You're going back to the castle aren't you?'

I nodded.

'Serena just needs a few more days' rest than they will all be able to go home.' He looked away from me. 'I'm going to the meadow. Come visit me later.'

I watched him climb down the ladder and go sit at the table with Eva and Jordan.

'He likes you,' Eva said.

'It won't work out though,' Jordan cut in. 'Ariella is from Mystic and he is here.'

'I'm not going back,' I whispered.

Jordan looked at me with shock and something else that I couldn't read, but Eva smiled at me as though she knew I would say that. Jordan went to say something but I cut in.

'I've always felt like a part of me was missing. But being here, I almost feel like I'm with her. I'm with my mum. I feel at home here. I feel complete, so I'm going to stay.'

Eva smiled at me. 'Go tell him that.'

I looked at her and saw full support in her eyes. I smiled back and walked over to the front door, climbing down the ladder to run to the meadow. I saw Hale sitting and talking to Laszlo and Samir. My heart was racing in my chest as I ran across the field. Hale stood when he saw me. I ran to him, throwing my arms around his neck and kissed him. He pulled me into him and kissed me back, more passionately than we'd ever kissed before.

'I'm yours,' I whispered. 'I'll come back soon, I have to go to the castle.'

I kissed him one last time, said goodbye to Laszlo and Samir and then walked back to the castle. When I reached the valley it felt like it had blossomed with life: the walls were covered in emerald green vines which were blooming with bright flowers and the black forest was gone, now replaced with a stone bridge and crystal blue water.

The sun was setting as I walked up the stairs to the front doors when I heard someone call my name. I turned around and saw Julius leaning on the bridge. I walked over to him and couldn't help but smile.

'The place looks much better. Your style is much more…less evil,' he said with a handsome smile.

I couldn't help it, but my eyes kept looking at his lips. 'Thank you,' I said, trying to keep eye contact. 'The dark forest wasn't my thing.'

He leant in and kissed me, pulling me up against his body and running his hands through my hair. My arms were around his neck as I melted into his kiss, a fire burning in my core.

I pulled away from him and take a step back, my heart racing in my chest.

'I can't,' I whispered. 'I'm with…'

He stepped towards me and put his head to mine. 'We are both immortal. That won't be the last time I kiss you.'

He kissed my cheek then turned and walked away into the night. I spun around and walked back up the stairs.

Walking through the castle doors Colt greeted me. 'I have sorted through the guards and most chose your allegiance in a heartbeat. Only half a dozen remained loyal to Jareth. They are down in the dungeons along with Chantelle, Jay and Jessica.'

I thanked him and then headed down to the dungeons. When I approached the bars they all stayed silent.

'What, nothing to say now that you're the ones in the cage?' I mocked.

Chantelle scowled at me, Jay ignored me but Jessica rose from where she sat and approached the bars. 'If you think this is the end princess, you're in for a rude awakening.'

I didn't respond to her threat and walked out of the dungeon, returning to the throne room and sitting upon my throne. It was so hard to get used to, I was Queen. It was unbelievable.

Jace and Nancy entered and bowed before me. 'Your Highness.'

'Don't bow to me,' I said. 'I feel weird having friends bow to me, so I forbid it.'

'You summoned us?' Nancy asked. I looked at her confused. I didn't remember doing that.

'I did,' said a voice from the door. We all looked and saw Arya standing there in black jeans and a short, dark blue midriff. At least she was clothed this time.

'Your Majesty,' the two elves said and bowed as she reached them. She held out a closed hand to each of them. As she opened her hands I saw a small glowing rock lying in each palm. They both looked at her in amazement as they took the rocks. I watched with fascination as the rocks formed into different animals; Nancy's turned into a tiger and Jace's was an otter.

'They are fallen stars,' Arya said, talking to me but still looking at Jace and Nancy. 'They take the form of the soul of the supernatural creature that possess it and lets out warnings when danger is near.'

'Where is…' Arya asked them softly, though I could still hear. 'She isn't with…'

'No,' Jace said. 'I'm returning home to her now. I promise you she is safe, and never with…'

Arya nods and turned back to me.

'It's nice to see you fully dressed,' I said as she stood before me.

She laughed.

'Why don't you ever look like royalty?' I asked her.

'Because I am like you,' she said meeting my eyes. 'I didn't ask for the throne. My mother Nefertiti was an elfish princess but when she married my father she got dethroned. I am prophesised so I got given her crown.'

She handed me a small black box. 'It is a lead box, keeps the power contained inside.'

I opened the box and looked at her in shock. It was the locket. I closed the lid and gasped at her. 'How did you get it? Jareth was thrown into oblivion.'

'I always had it,' she said with guilt. 'Just before you were born your mother asked me to retrieve it. That's how my relationship with your brother begun – I needed to steal his blood in order to retrieve the locket.'

'Why didn't you tell me?' I exclaimed.

'Because then you wouldn't have risen to the throne. You needed to do this,' she said with a nervous smile. 'Now shall we do this?'

I looked at her confused.

'You promised Nancy to help her get her sister back. I am here to accompany you so we should get going. It's a long journey to the unclaimed lands.'

CHAPTER THIRTY-ONE

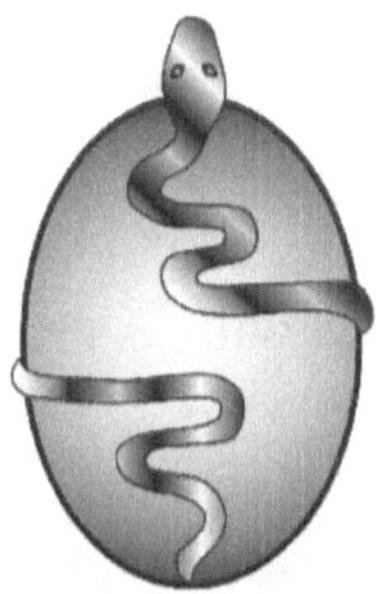

I looked at Arya who was standing at the door ready to go. She had a small satchel, her weapons belt equipped with a sword and a few daggers, the bow, arrows and two more swords on her back and a long black coat wrapped around her. She looked like she was going on a hunting trip not a mission into some unknown lands.

I looked at the bag I carried and wondered if I needed more essential items. I had a few bottles of water, some food bars, toilet paper, bandages, plus my weapons already strapped on.

'Why are you wearing a coat?' I called out to Arya. 'It's barely cold out.'

She looked at me with annoyed look for making her wait. 'We are going into the unclaimed lands,' she said bluntly. 'The realm of vampires, ghosts and all creatures of the dark. It's going to be cold.'

Oh. I realised I didn't actually know anything about the unclaimed lands, and was now wishing I still didn't know because I was less than thrilled to be venturing into it now. I walked to the cloak room and grabbed out a red coat and wrapped it around myself.

When I walked back to the front door of my castle I saw both Nancy and Arya waiting for me. I supressed a sigh and walked over to them.

'I'm ready,' I said with as much confidence as I could muster.

Arya led us through the maze and to the hill top where I first began my original quest. I looked around. The only thing up here with us was an old tree. I went to ask where we were going but Arya held her hand up to silence me. I looked back at my castle but found myself staring at a brown wall, we were in Styr's.

He came out of his office and greeted us with a bow.

'What can I do for you ladies?' he asked.

'We need to go into the unclaimed lands,' Arya said with command.

Styr shook his head. 'I will not allow it.'

Arya rolled her eyes. 'Cut the hippy crap Styr, we need to enter, it's a rescue mission.'

He stood dangerously close before her. I held my breath at the tension. She kept her eyes looking into his and he broke a smile.

'I won't,' he said and took a step back.

Nancy stepped forward. 'Please, I need to save my little sister.'

Styr looked at her and sighed. 'I'll let you out on the mountain side but you cross over into the darkness alone.'

We walked back to the door to exited onto the mountain side. I nodded at Styr in thanks then turned to walk out.

'You won't like what you find Arya,' Styr yelled out as Arya closed the door behind us.

We walked up the mountain side. I kept an eye on my footing not wanting to fall over or down the mountain. I pulled out a bottle of water and drank half of it in one gulp and poured some over my head. It was so hot from the sun and the walking, despite Arya saying it was going to be cold. We reached the top of the mountain and I gasped at the view. The land looked haunted and dangerous but the sun setting in the distance was a beautiful sight. As darkness engulfed the land I noticed a blue mist still covered part of the view.

'The graveyards where the ghosts linger,' Arya said answering my unasked question. 'The werewolves are on the mountain side, the dark elves in the forest among other things, the ghosts are where the blue mist is but the question is where do the vampires hide?'

'I thought vampires were good,' I asked.

'They are…mostly,' Arya said as we continued down the mountain. 'But some chose to give up their soul and from that there is no going back.'

'How do they give up their soul?'

Arya glanced back at Nancy, then back to me. 'They take a human life.'

'But why?'

Arya sighed. 'Some do it for power, some do it because they fall in love with someone from the darkness, or some just by accident. When vampires are first turned they need blood. For some the blood lust is so strong they accidently kill their first victim.'

Nancy and Arya suddenly stopped in the tracks. I looked around and wondered why they stopped. I opened my mouth but Arya shushed me. I looked to Nancy who mouthed *werewolves* at me. I placed my hand on the hilt of my sword and looked around. Arya signalled us to follow her. She moved silently down the mountain and we followed in step.

As Arya knelt to the ground I peered around the mountain side to see a man standing in a circle of wolves. I felt panicked. Was he in danger? The wolves ran off and he looked up at the moon, sniffing. He looked around until his red eyes met mine, smiling a devilish grin. I then watched the horrible sight as his body transformed into a wolf.

He howled and suddenly all the wolves were back at his side.

I felt Arya pull on my arm and I turned to see Nancy already running down the mountain. I followed Arya and tried to keep up. I could hear the wolves still howling. We reached the bottom of the mountain but I looked up and saw the wolves running down.

Arya pulled out an arrow and aimed it at the wolves.

'You can't shoot them all,' I yelled as she released the arrow. It pierced just below the heart of the wolf with red eyes.

'I missed on purpose,' she yelled to the wolves, who had all stopped to surround their injured brother. 'Hunt us again and I will put the next arrow between your alpha's eyes.'

The wolves growled at us in anger but began to return up the mountain. The one with red eyes turned back into a man and pulled the arrow out. His eyes flashed with anger but he too turned and went back up.

We walked into the woods that resided at the bottom of the mountain. I had an eerie feeling that I was being watched. We came to a small clearing and stopped to make camp for the night. I hugged the coat around me and was now thankful for bringing it. We didn't risk lighting a fire because Arya said too many dark creatures resided in the woods. We did not need the attention.

'I suppose you would like to know why we are venturing through the unclaimed lands,' Nancy said softly.

Arya and I both looked at her but remained silent.

'Lydia, my younger sister was travelling through the forest on the other side of the mountain when she went missing. I didn't leave that forest for over a week. A few days after returning home I received a note. Vampires from the unclaimed lands had claimed her, was all it said.'

'You should have called me straight away,' Arya said.

'I didn't want to bother you. I thought you were back in the mortal realm,' Nancy said.

'I was,' Arya said, rubbing her hands together and breathing in to them to warm them up. 'I came back because I sensed Ariella was in pain.' She looked at me. I threw her a look of confusion. 'We have a blood connection,' she said bluntly.

'What's a blood connection?' I asked.

'My father and mother are different breeds, which makes it impossible for them to conceive but my mother did so your mother gave her a daily dosage of her blood all through the pregnancy and then me until the age of six.'

'How'd they conceive?' I asked.

'Well my mother had a near death experience, and your mother gave her a potion which also had her blood in it. It must have allowed her organs to become pregnant with me – anyway I have your mother's blood and power so I can sense your pain.'

We stretched out on the cold dirt and closed our eyes, attempting sleep. I dozed off and minutes later got woken by Nancy's scream. We were surrounded. Nancy was already pinned to the ground. I reached for my sword but stopped when I saw Arya standing with her hands up in defeat. I looked at who surrounded us and saw they look similar to Nancy but different: black hair and black eyes. These must be the dark elves that Arya mentioned.

They pulled me to my feet and then walked us through the forest. 'Where are they taking us?' I whispered to Arya.

Before Arya answered we reached a castle made out of trees. Even though we were in serious trouble I couldn't stop myself from gasping at the beauty. We were pushed through the doors and up the stairs into a small throne room.

A dark elf with long blonde hair stood before us, his back to us. His blonde hair had black foils and braids running through it. He turned around and looked us over with his deep, black eyes. I held my breath and looked away so I didn't hold eye contact.

He walked over to Arya. I saw her looking down to avoid his gaze also. He stroked the hair back from her face, and a devilish smile crept onto his lips.

'Your Highness,' he said in a sickeningly velvet voice. 'Welcome to my kingdom. Though it is without a queen, I have heard of the darkness and chaos you have caused. Will you join me?'

Arya quickly grabbed her sword and swung it at the elf, but he was quicker. He grabbed the blade of her sword and it turned to ash. Waving his hand and the guards to grab us again, they dragged us down the stairs, and down into the dungeon. Arya in one cell; Nancy and I in the other.

'Now what?' I asked as the guards walked away, leaving only one elf watching us. They must have faith in their dungeons.

Arya winked at me and leant on her bars. I watched her with amazement as she muttered a spell under her breath. Her lips glowed bright red for a moment and then returned to normal. When she opened her eyes they were black. She stripped off her coat and walked to the front of the cell.

'If I knew there were elves as sexy as you here I would have been caught long ago,' she said to the elf guarding us. I rolled my eyes at her obvious flirting.

He looked her over with hunger. She stretched which made her singlet pull up above her belly button. He walked over to her cage and she put her arms through the bars and around his waist. He leaned in and kissed her. The minute his lips touched hers he fell unconscious and Arya stood there holding the keys to the cell.

'A simple sleep charm,' she said shrugging her shoulders. I noticed her eyes were back to blue as she unlocked her cell then came and unlocked ours.

Nancy took the lead and we followed her out of the castle and back into the forest. We kept running until we were out of the trees and back onto open land. I felt too exposed out here though. I looked back at the forest and wondered if the elves were still watching us.

'We have to find a graveyard,' Nancy said. 'The ghost will know where the vampires are.'

I pointed in the distance where I saw blue mist. 'Arya, didn't you say the ghost resided in the blue stuff?'

We continued walking and I resisted complaining about how sore my feet were. 'It can't still be night, can it?' I asked, feeling as though we had been here for hours.

'It's always dark here,' Nancy said without turning around.

We reached the graveyard and I was startled by the sight. The blue mist wasn't mist; it was the ghosts. There were beyond thousands of them wandering around, all blue and transparent.

'Excuse me?' Nancy asked a ghost passing us; he turned to look at her with his one eye, the other hidden beneath an eye patch. He even had a parrot on his shoulder.

'Aye me lady,' he said with a croaky voice. 'What does the lady wish?'

'I am looking for the vampires.'

'Why do you want t' find them? Horrible creatures if you ask me.'

'They kidnapped my sister.'

'Kill them all I say. They be six hundred paces west.'

We thanked the pirate ghost and continued west. I silently counted my steps as we walked. As I reached five hundred I looked up and saw a house that looked to be falling down. And of course that was a hundred paces ahead and our destination.

Nancy walked quietly up to the front door and pushed it open. It creaked softly but no other sound was made. I followed her inside and we walked up the stairs in search of her sister. Arya stayed on the ground floor and looked for any vampires lurking around. Nancy and I looked in every room on the second floor but they were all empty. We ventured up to the third floor. The first door we opened I saw a young blonde girl handcuffed against the wall. Nancy ran to her and unchained her. I ran to her side and helped her carry the girl. We made it to the bottom of the stairs but the door was blocked by vampires.

Arya was thrown into the room by a vampire she must have been fighting with in the other room. She pulled the two swords from her back and started slashing at every vampire that came within arm's reach. I put Lydia's full weight on Nancy and pulled out my sword to help Arya, a gap opening up to the door way. I fought my way to the exit and called for Nancy to run as I kept the vampires back. Once Nancy was out the door with Lydia I called to Arya.

I looked over at her and saw she had stopped fighting. She was staring at the vampire walking towards her. He had shoulder length blonde hair with a braid keeping it back from his face. His eyes were black and his fangs were out.

'I'm surprised to see you my love,' the blonde vampire said to Arya.

'Quinn...' escaped Arya's lips.

'Arya, let's go,' I called from the door, keeping my eyes on the vampires still in the room, even though they had stopped fighting.

'I'll see you soon my love,' Quinn said to Arya before he turned around and walked up the stairs.

Arya turned on her heels and finally followed me out. We didn't stop walking until we neared the graveyard again. Nancy sat her sister down and then walked over to Arya and I.

'Did you kill him?' Nancy asked Arya.

'Did you know he was here?' Arya yelled.

Nancy flinched. 'I had a feeling.'

'What is going on?' I asked. 'Arya, are you okay?'

'No,' she said, her voice sounded close to breaking. 'I didn't kill him, you know I can't,' she said to Nancy then turned away from us and walked into the night.

'Arya,' I called out.

'She won't come back,' Nancy said.

'Why not?' I argued.

'The blonde vampire in there, she used to have a connection with him. Just leave it at that,' she said then turned to her sister. I looked into the night where Arya had walked off but there was no sign of her.

CHAPTER THIRTY-TWO

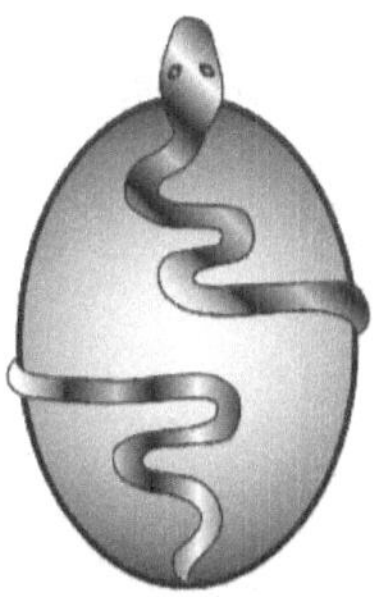

It was sunrise as we reached Alesmera again. I sighed in relief to be out of those cursed lands. I took off the coat and just carried it the rest of the journey. Nancy bid me farewell as we reached the maze and I continued to my castle.

I walked straight to the chamber I had claimed as my room and went to the bedside table, pulling out the lead box that Arya had given me containing the necklace. I wanted to open it but resisted the urge. I put it back in the drawer then walked out of my room and to my throne room.

I went up and sat in my chair. The doors were open and so were the front doors, giving me a beautiful view of my kingdom. I watched the last few seconds of the sunset.

Colt walked in and bowed before me.

'Your Majesty.' He handed me a letter. 'This arrived for you in your absence.'

'Thank you Colt,' I said taking it.

He bowed again before exiting the room.

I opened the letter and almost dropped it after reading it:

Don't get used to your throne
- Aubrey

Acknowledgements

'Waiting for a dream is like waiting for a falling star'

For as long as I could remember I've loved writing, it's kept me sane but without the support of my friends and family, my dream of being published would never have happened.

I want to thank my Dad, my Mum and my brother, Riley. Thank you for all those times I would steal the computer from you before I got my own laptop and always believing that I could do this. I love you.

Thank you to all of my crazy but amazing family, you have all always been so supportive of my dreams, you've always asked me how my writing is going and encouraging me.

Thank you to my amazing friends and family friend who have always been so supportive towards me.

A big shout out to my Alice in Wonderland best friends, you know who you are. I could not have got this far without you in my life, you guys are my rock, the loves of my life.

Now without these people the publishing process would never have happened.

Thank you to Simon, Nancy and Phoenix for reading the early drafts of my stories, they have probably changed heaps since then.

Ashleigh – thank you and your red pen, I always loved reading what you thought and editing what you said needed fixing, just thank you for being an awesome editor, I really trust your judgement.

Wayne – thank you for the completely gorgeous cover work you did for me. And for Kimberley, if you hadn't made her cover so amazing I may not have stopped and bought her book, and I am so glad I did.

Kimberley – thank you for all your awesome advice and answering my silly questions. And thank you for introducing me to Erin, and what a Beta Reader even was.

Erin – thank you for reading over my manuscript, I look forward to working with you in the future.

Sabrina - where do I start, I had no idea what I was doing, the whole publishing process was doing my head in more than writing the manuscript was, thank you for helping me take that last step. I am very excited to continue working with you in the future.

Cover Design by Wayne Nichols © 2016
www.wnichols.com

Map by Amber Morant © 2016
www.ambermorant.com

Find us at

www.facebook.com/ouroborusbooks

and

www.facebook/danicapecknovels